ANYTHING FOR THE DEVIL

THE FIRST DEAL

AURORA GRAVES

WEATHERVANE
— PRESS —

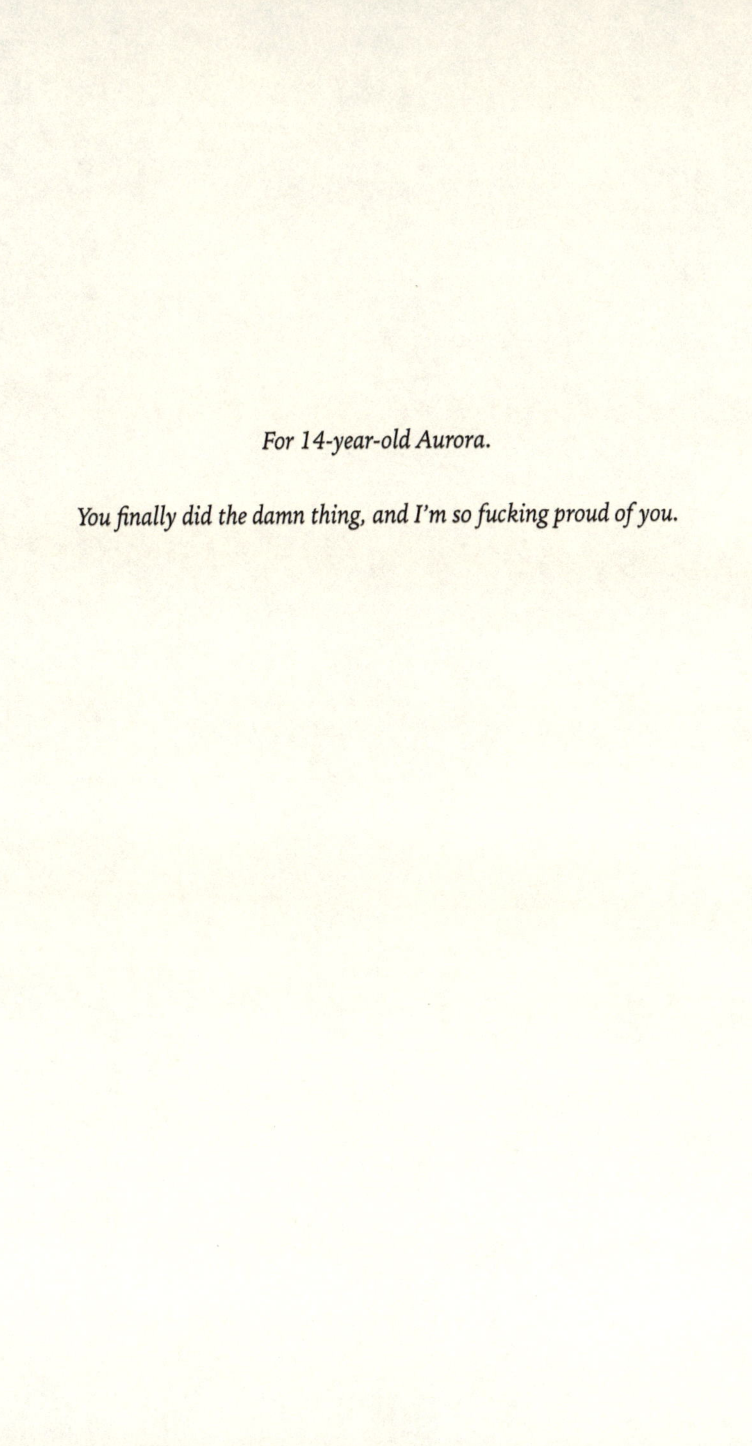

For 14-year-old Aurora.

You finally did the damn thing, and I'm so fucking proud of you.

Contents & Playlist

You may all go to hell, and I will go to Texas.

— Davy Crockett

CHAPTER 1

WELCOME HOME

–HellYeah

STAGE LIGHTS WHIRL OVER THE CROWD, HYPNOTIC blue and green and magenta highlighting a sea of devil horns and arms waving back and forth to the beat of a metalcore song. Four bodies move on one of the smallest stages available in San Antonio and headbang along with fans singing and screaming lyrics right back to them.

My fingers tap the same chords against my thigh like I've got strings and a fretboard in hand.

Like I haven't gone a year and a half without playing.

Adrian, ever shirtless and displaying an assortment of new tattoos, breaks a drumstick on swinging cymbals. Half of it whizzes past heads into the crowd. He grimaces and reaches for a new one at the side of his set without missing a beat.

His twin brother Zak pulls away from a girl trying to yank him off stage while shredding his guitar. A cymbal stand jerks when he takes a couple of steps back and runs into it.

My brother Robbie keeps running into Shannon, threatening to impale the tall and lanky vocalist on the neck of his bass or kick him off the stage entirely.

Adrian's other drumstick splits in two and dings Robbie on the head.

Robbie spins around and shouts something unintelligible beneath Shannon's screams cutting through the atmosphere. Adrian's mouth puckers into an angry frown, and he gives Robbie a tattooed middle finger as his other hand wails on a china cymbal.

Robbie stops playing entirely.

He yanks the strap over his head, seizes the neck of his shimmering blue Ibanez bass in both hands, and hammers it right into the shattered clock printed on the kick drum.

An ear-piercing shriek slices through the speakers and the music screeches to a halt.

"Fuck you!"

Adrian leaps over his kit and cymbals fall. Metal crashes and clangs against the hard surface of the stage, sending an electrical surge of goosebumps through my skin.

Robbie throws the first punch, but Adrian ducks and bum rushes his shoulder into Robbie's gut. My brother is slightly taller and definitely stockier than Adrian, but the drummer's lean figure packs serious muscle from drumming since he realized he could bang sticks against shit to make noise. The way Robbie visibly loses his breath when he flies into the side stage wall from the sheer brute force makes me cringe.

Shannon hurries to tug his brother-in-law off Robbie, but Zak elbows Shannon aside. His long hair is already tied up on top of his head and tattooed arms with new muscles are ready to kick ass the second he grabs Robbie, slams him to the floor, and pummels the shit out of him alongside Adrian.

Shannon takes a couple of steps back, scrubbing a hand over his face. His shaggy blond hair clings to his sweaty forehead and frames a look of irritation.

He must've realized they're still in the middle of a gig

when his hazel eyes sweep over the crowd. His lips move, saying, "Oh, shit," before bringing the mic to his lips. "Sorry, y'all. Looks like the show's over."

The crowd groans and jeers. A couple of long-time fans I recognize toss plastic cups of beer at the fighting trio before climbing on stage to try and break things up, themselves.

Shannon notices me in the back, his expression flickering between excitement, disbelief, and shame before he mouths, "I'm sorry."

"Jesus fucking Christ," I mutter under my breath, wondering where the fuck everything went so wrong.

Brandy leans toward me and says loudly, "I told you it was bad."

I knock back the rest of my beer and turn away. "I'll see you at Mom's."

I don't bother looking back, leaving the shouting and racket behind as the doors close.

The deep breath I take outside in downtown San Antonio is anything but refreshing in the stifling summer heat. It's not as humid as where I just arrived from, but it is a hell of a lot hotter, making sweat form and collect in all the uncomfortable places. I tie up my long blond hair in a messy bun to let the sweaty back of my neck air out as I head a couple of blocks down to the parking lot to grab my car.

My phone buzzes and pings in my hand right as I reach my blue Honda Civic that's in desperate need of some TLC after the long-ass drive. The face that pops up on screen is the last one I saw in Atlanta who demanded one more Waffle House date before I headed out, even if it was four in the morning.

Make it in one piece?

I start texting back as I climb into the car.

Yeah. Miss me already?

Ty barely gives me enough time to start the engine and turn the radio on to the shitty local rock station before responding.

You have no idea. You can have a week or two of vacation but imma need you to come back to ATL.

I smile wistfully at his text.

Duty calls with the family business and I know you understand that. You'll be OK without me.

I take another deep breath before putting the car into drive that helps bring me back home, taking my brain out of Atlanta and back into San Antonio. But it also renews the sour frown from watching the Ramos twins tag-teaming my older brother, their supposed BFF since religious education back in fourth grade.

Maybe if I had told Shannon I was coming back home they would've been on their best behavior and tonight wouldn't have been a shit show.

My hands wring the steering wheel. *It's not your fault they're all hotheaded.*

I wanted to see what the deal is for myself, anyway. Brandy has tried keeping me updated on band drama, filling me in on what Shannon and Robbie fail to mention, but it's gone in one ear and out the other.

I left it all behind for a reason, and I didn't want to hear about it.

But that was before last month when Shannon called.

Before Robbie and the twins were arrested for disorderly

conduct at their show in Atlanta that I skipped. Before I saw their battered mugshots in Metal Music News.

By the time Mom called a week later offering the creative director position at our family's New year's rock music festival, New Year's Ball, the second she offered to pay for breaking my lease was the moment I started packing.

Yet seeing the Ramos twins in the flesh has me considering driving past Losoya and heading all the way to Corpus Christi.

A solo trip to the coast to keep home at bay.

To keep Timeless and my past mistakes at bay.

A new text message alert pings through the speakers and startles me. I tap the screen to listen.

"New message from Ty Blackburn: 'So what you're telling me is it's my turn to come to you?' Would you like to reply?"

"Yes." I snort. "Your funeral, dude."

With the way the impending twilight darkens from clouds rolling in, the more it feels like my own funeral is approaching the closer I get to home.

As if she knew I was itching to keep going straight on 281, Mom's name pops up on the entertainment center screen and interrupts the music blaring through the speakers.

I swallow a smart-ass response that would cue her in on my potential escape plan. "Hey, I'm on my way now. Y'all need anything from the store?"

"You read my mind, baby girl," Mom replies. "Mind picking up extra beer for your daddy? Looks like Robbie got into it last time he was here."

That explains some things.

"Sure thing. Anything else?"

"Just yourself, baby."

The dollar store on the way is dirty, dim, claustrophobic, and haphazardly stocked as it was the day I left. A Hot

Cheetos display is front and center, right across from a Big Red end cap.

I'm definitely back in SA.

But Ty's response tries to coax me back into Atlanta.

> Idgaf. You seemed happier here and that's all I want. Well that and for you to not be so damn far away anymore xP Got used to seeing you all the time and I liked it.

My gaze drifts to the row of snacks in front of me, phone buzzing from gripping it so tightly.

If Ty thinks I was happy, then it's only further proof of why it was time for me to go.

Dirty Peach Studios kept me busy almost twenty-four seven since the day I stepped foot through the glass door, and whatever time I had left was spent with the guy I've known since we were in diapers. But it was just that: keeping me busy.

Keeping my mind off Timeless, the Ramos twins, and my fuck up of the century.

I blink the thought away and reach for a twenty-four pack of Lone Star.

Maybe hooking up with Ty wasn't my brightest idea, but it wasn't the worst mistake I've made, either. Nothing is technically bad about the guy besides the occasional flare of temper and being a bit jealous at times.

It seems no matter where I go that I'm the problem.

The smile I force when I come face to face with Gigi, an old classmate and one of Zak's ex-girlfriends from high school, turns genuine when she beams at me brightly. She's the same as ever with her dark hair slicked back into a neat bun and big hoop earrings grazing her shoulders.

"Hey, stranger," she greets. "Long time, no see."

"Yeah, I just got back into town," I tell her as she scans

the beer. "And I just remembered I can have breakfast tacos in the morning."

Gigi chuckles. "Always a plus. When'd you get back?"

"Couple hours ago. Haven't gone by my parents' yet."

Gigi sets the twenty-four pack atop the bagging carousel, staring out the door. "They're over by the creek still, right?"

"Yeah. Why?"

She hesitates before saying, "I think it's some bored kids, but there's been some weird stuff going on at the approach."

I groan. "Are they doin' that Devil's Bridge shit again? They always get the wrong bridge—"

"The bridge don't matter. People can summon up anything regardless."

"What's been going on?"

"I've seen a lot of stuff left on the approach that look like offerings. Sometimes there's blood, but there hasn't been a dead animal left behind. Maybe a coyote gets to them before morning."

"Guess some kids are desperate to get the hell out of school and graduate, huh?" I reach for the beer. "Someone should probably tell 'em selling their soul to the devil for good grades isn't worth it."

Gigi tuts. "I'm serious. Bad things happen when they start leaving stuff like that. There's no telling what could pop up."

I imitate a claw with my free hand. "Maybe la lechuza's gonna swoop down and scare 'em straight, huh?"

"Ay, Stephani!" she exclaims, crossing herself and kissing the cross she makes with her thumb and forefinger. "Don't say that!"

Snorting, I amble toward the door. "C'mon, Gigi. Don't be a scaredy cat. I bet it's just bored-ass kids wantin' to stir up a little trouble. No devil or lechuza's gonna get nobody."

"Just keep on the lookout, alright?"

Devil's Bridge is nothing but a creepy legend that every

town has. San Antonio's lucky to have more than one. But, in Losoya, people always go to the abandoned approach next to Losoya Bridge over the river—which is the wrong bridge, either way.

"Maybe it is just a bunch of bored kids. But there's no telling."

My weight shifts from foot to foot with the glass door pressed to my back. Finally, I nod. "Okay. I'll watch out."

Gigi pauses for a split second. "I know we weren't close in high school, but it's still nice seein' you."

I flash a smile. "Good seein' you, too."

San Antonio illuminates the dark sky despite the rural-ness of Losoya, so the stars here in Texas aren't so big and bright. The last streetlight before the road to home is the one at the bridge, and the inky blackness that settles over the area says it's busted.

I ease off the gas to slow down a little and check for road-side offerings or anything suspicious on the abandoned approach beside the bridge. But there aren't even any small memorials for accidents, never mind ritual offerings for the devil or whatever else those kids might be trying to summon.

Something flashes in my periphery above the bridge, where the approach stands watch over the river.

I gasp, clutching my chest and trying not to swerve into the water rushing below.

An owl flaps its gigantic wingspan in the outermost part of my car's headlights before passing over and heading west.

After double checking that it's not actually the witch-owl of legend following me for poking fun, I chuckle and flip the blinker to turn onto the road to home.

Nearly everyone in San Antonio has their own lechuza story; either their abuela or drunk tio or even the person telling the story has seen the man-eating owl with their own eyes. I grew up hearing the stories and watching my classmates give each other goosebumps and nightmares to carry with them throughout the day, swearing stay inside after dark.

But out here in the rural south side of San Antonio, there are no lechuzas or devils—just spooky shadows, busted streetlights, and the ghosts of my past.

CHAPTER 2

THE ONE YOU LEFT BEHIND

—VAYDEN

IT MIGHT BE DARK OUT, BUT THE DARKNESS CAN'T swallow the golden light splaying over the pavement leading to my parents' house.

Mom's really outdone herself with lights strung up all across the yard and lanterns lighting the way, like she put them all out here to guide me home. Or maybe the shadows that the live oaks and pecan trees cast over the house have finally creeped her out enough.

My usual parking spot across from the pecan tree is wide open. Mom and Dad both are already rushing out the front door to greet me.

Mom squeezes me extra hard. "You're early! Concert get too wild?"

I choke back a sarcastic laugh. "Yeah, it got a little out of hand." I throw my arms around Dad's neck before handing over the beer. "Ran into Gigi down at the store. She said she's been seeing stuff at the approach?"

Dad grunts, beer in one hand and one of my suitcases in the other as he leads us up the porch stairs and into the house. "Your mama's been keepin' me busy with all her projects. I wouldn't know either way."

Even the inside of the house has been all spruced up and rearranged. When they usher me into my old bedroom, though, it's exactly as I left it almost two years ago: same floral bedspread, same bedside lamp and desk, same rock band posters pinned to the wall. Where a Timeless poster used to hang now displays my high school diploma.

"Surprised you didn't go hog wild redecorating in here, too," I comment as I place a suitcase on the desk.

"Why would I?"

"Because I don't live here anymore?"

"Well, you do now, don't you?"

Sighing, I relent, "Just until I can find my own place."

"You can stay here as long as you want, you know. Miss having you here."

"I know. Thank you."

I busy myself situating suitcases on the floor and bed, but Mom stops me, hugging me even more tightly than before.

"We're really glad you're home, Steph. Missed you so much." She chuckles under her breath. "New Year's Ball hasn't been the same without you here squealing about the next surprise band."

I hug her back, but my heart isn't really in it. It's enough to make her leave me be, saying that they'll be out back.

At least Mom kept up dusting in here. I can't imagine how thick it would be after a year and a half.

I have to sit on the edge of the bed.

I wonder how much everything has changed. If the rock music festival my parents started so many years ago has changed at all from the one time in my life I haven't attended. If Shannon's daughter, Zak and Adrian's niece, is just as small as I remember her. If the twins' older sister,

Shannon's wife, Kris kept up with Wednesday puzzle nights for Andrea since I've been gone.

I swallow the bitterness those thoughts leave behind and perk up when Mom calls, "Stephani, come on and make yourself a plate before those boys eat up everything!"

I'll let her figure it out when only two of the guys show up.

The patio is the same with the wooden beams covering it, but there's new furniture and an entire garden complete with a winding pathway around the pool. It leads to a cozy corner with more furniture around a firepit and a waterfall feature behind that. More lights are strung up through the trees. They've embraced the cactus, too, using different patches as décor around the waterfall and leading out back toward the woods.

"Holy crap," I breathe, taking a paper plate when Mom offers it. "You've been keeping Dad super busy, huh?"

Dad grumbles under his breath, flipping burgers on the grill. Mom smacks his shoulder with a stack of plates. "Oh, hush. Looks nice, don't it?"

Headlights flash across the trees, catching my attention with the sound of an approaching vehicle.

"You better hurry and grab all the pasta salad you want before your brother sniffs it out," Dad comments, watching me doing just that.

I know Mom said they both missed me, but I think Dad's being a tough sell right now with the distant look in his eyes.

Kissing his cheek on my way to the table seems to warm him up a little.

Another set of headlights illuminates the dark trees. Must be Shannon, I think, until another vehicle rumbles in behind that.

Brandy and Robbie round the corner hand in hand.

"Wow, you actually stuck around," Robbie comments loudly.

"I'm second guessing the decision," I murmur into his ear as he envelops me in a bear hug.

He pulls away, unable to hide the shame even under dim lights. "I'm sorry."

I glance over his shoulder at the figure that stepped up onto the patio. Shannon's face lights up the second he sees me, and I can't help returning the beam. "Who else came?"

"Everyone."

My eyes bug out of their sockets. "*What?*"

Robbie's face is suddenly in mine. Where his septum piercing normally sits is caked with dried blood. "Nobody's gonna say shit, alright? Play it cool."

"Shit about what?" I hiss before he spins around and heads toward the grill after Brandy.

Forget the fight on stage for a second—I don't want to see either of the Ramos twins.

"Hey, Steph," Shannon whoops, pulling me into a hug. He lowers his voice. "Sorry for the shit homecoming gig. They promised to behave here, at least."

My head starts to shake and I turn away. "I can't be here with them."

Shannon grabs my arm, making me crane my head back since he's so tall. "Just ignore them, okay? You have to stay." He cocks his chin toward the grill. "For your parents. Not for them."

I didn't think my expression could fall any further than it already has, but one glimpse at Mom smiling over at Dad and Robbie before grinning at me is all the guilt it takes to force me to sit back down.

But my skin crawls wondering who else pulled in.

The appetite I had suddenly disappears. I stare at my half-full plate until another figure appears around the corner.

Adrian.

Seeing the eldest of the Ramos twins doesn't help me breathe any easier. Especially not when he gives Robbie a death glare over Mom's shoulder as he hugs her.

His attention comes to me, and his jaw drops.

"Steph, what the hell are you doin' here?" Adrian exclaims as he rushes toward me. He sweeps me up into a hug that forces my arms around his neck to regain balance, but I go rigid in his arms. His body pressing against mine sends me reeling backwards.

I chuckle uncomfortably under my breath. He smells like sweat and beer, and he's more muscular than I remember.

A distant, buried memory appears, smelling of the same sweat and beer and an extra strong stench of pot, the same sound of crickets pounding in my head when I realized…

I all but shove him away, saying, "Thought it was about time I came back home."

"Yeah, now that you're the big wig creative director for NYB, huh?" He holds me by the shoulders, taking in the sight of me. "You're different."

Eyeballing his low-fade black hair, gold nose ring, and the grayscale floral tattoo creeping up his neck from under his shirt, I reply, "So are you, mister."

Beaming, his hands slip from my shoulders. They linger around mine for a moment before he clears his throat and releases. "Yeah, a bit. Maybe it wouldn't be so drastic if you'd've stayed."

I stare at him silently for an uncomfortable moment. "Go fix yourself a plate."

He stares back helplessly. When he finally turns away and Mom hands him a plate, he does a double take over his shoulder—I guess making sure I haven't disappeared into thin air yet.

Mom and Brandy flank either side of me at the end of the

table, and even though I pick up my burger, I'm still distracted, staring at the end of the patio and wondering if someone else will round the corner.

I'm so focused that I jump when Mom pats my arm.

"Brandy, I bet you're glad Steph is finally home."

"Yes!" she exclaims, nudging my shoulder roughly. "'Bout time, huh?"

The guys settle at the table and Mom continues, "How was your trip, anyway? Bet you're glad to be out of Hotlanta."

A sad smile tugs at the corners of my lips, but the unsureness of being back home in the middle of everyone I've disappointed the most stops a response from me.

The only disappointment I created in Atlanta was from telling Dave I was going back to NYB full time and Ty I was coming back home to San Antonio.

It's not until I clear thickening melancholy from my throat that I can say anything at all. "I'll miss Waffle House somethin' awful, but I think breakfast taco country is where I belong."

Everyone clamors all at once in rabid agreement—even Robbie and Adrian agree.

Laughter bubbles out of me until I catch movement at the end of the patio, looking to meet a familiar, golden-brown gaze.

My heart sinks.

The last time I saw Zak, we were screaming at each other in the driveway—me telling him I quit the band and was moving, and him demanding that I stay and talk things through.

Before that, he got down on one knee on stage at New Year's Ball in front of a crowd of adoring fans.

And I told him no.

Chapter 3

Pain

—Dry Kill Logic

I didn't see that extra special New Year's Ball concert coming.

Zak wasn't supposed to stop the show, or pull me to center stage. He wasn't supposed to drop down on one knee; the entire crowd wasn't supposed to hoot and holler in excitement.

Then again, I wasn't supposed to betray the love of my life, either.

After leaving town the way I did, after hooking up with someone else, I probably shouldn't care anymore about the heartbreak that appeared on Zak's face when I chose to run out of his life.

But when he comes to a halt and realization sets in, the wound is ripped open, gushing with fresh, feverous blood that makes me choke.

Running away didn't do a goddamn thing.

"Zak!"

Mom scrambles and rushes over, giving him a big mom hug only she can give. "We weren't too sure if you were gonna come by."

She pats his bearded cheek, finally making him break our stare down as he focuses on her face through oversized gold frame glasses.

When he smiles, I have to look away.

Mom shoos him on to make himself a plate before coming back to my side and reaching for my hand.

I snatch it away, glaring at her before averting my gaze to my mostly-empty plate.

It suddenly disappears, and Brandy grabs my hand.

"C'mon, Steph," she starts, rising from the table. "Let's go make some drinks. You want one, Mom?"

Once she pulls me inside the house and into the kitchen, I take a deep breath before letting it loose.

"What the *fuck* is he doing here?" Stealing a peep through the window and eyeballing his head illuminated by dim string lights, I mutter, "And what the fuck is up with those douchebag glasses? Goddamn hipster."

Brandy snorts as she grabs ingredients for margaritas. "I don't think he expected you to be here."

I throw my hands in the air. "He's my ex. Why the hell would he show up here, anyway?"

She lines up glasses on the counter. "Mom and Dad are the only parents the twins have. And, hell, Zak still goes with them to Our Lady every Sunday. Same Mass, every single week."

Grunting, I cross my arms and lean against the counter. "Still doesn't make things any less weird."

"Either way, he's here. You don't have to acknowledge him." Brandy points at the window behind me overlooking the backyard. "Mom's got that cozy little corner we can sequester ourselves to."

"I'm gonna need, like, two pitchers to get through this. And what about the guys?"

"Shannon put on his dad hat and told 'em all to be on

their best behavior. Think they'll be fine the rest of the night, anyway. Something about fistfighting gets it outta their system for a little while."

"So, about a month?" I say incredulously.

"Funny, isn't it, that Timeless didn't have problems until after you quit," she responds with a flat tone before dumping tequila into a pitcher.

The urge to scrub a hand over my face is intense as tequila *glug-glug-glugs*, but I ball up my hand to save my makeup. "I did everyone a favor."

The bottle clanks against the counter as Brandy turns to glare at me. Upset flares in her eyes. "By leaving town and cutting everyone out when you decided you were too chicken shit to commit to your boyfriend? Brilliant plan. Ten outta ten—nothin' else could've done better."

Crossing my arms, I lean back against a cabinet and watch her stir ingredients. After a moment, I finally say, "I'm sorry."

She tuts. "Right."

I scoff back at her. "Hey, you know, I've been talkin' to you this entire time—"

"Because *I've* been the one reaching out," she responds curtly. "The couple times I tried letting it go, we didn't talk for months. Literal months."

As much as I want to argue about it, I keep my trap shut.

I escaped to Atlanta for a reason: to get away, start fresh, and keep myself busy. I let Dirty Peach musicians keep me as busy as they would let me so I didn't have to call or text home often—I didn't want to answer questions about why I left, when I was going to come visit, if I'd come back home soon.

Coming clean would've made me a lot more enemies than quitting Timeless and leaving town the way I did.

After pouring and setting the pitcher aside, Brandy turns to face me. She's a tiny little thing, but she's been my best girl friend for ever—I know when there's a rage brewing inside.

"I thought we were best friends, Steph," she finally says. "You were my sister from another mister. My future sister-in-law when Rob grows the balls to ask me."

"You're still my best friend," I interrupt quickly.

A grimace forms on her face, and she slowly shakes her head. "No, I'm not. Best friends get on FaceTime just to hang out, no talking necessary. Best friends are there for each other when shit hits the fan and we feel like we can't get out of bed anymore. We don't just let them figure it all out on their own—"

I throw my arms around her, hugging her closely and trying my best to blink back tears. I haven't even been back in town but for a couple of hours—I can't let the waterworks start now.

A tear slips down my nose.

Fuck.

I snivel against her shoulder. "I'm really sorry."

She pushes me away, refusing to even look at me as she hands me a glass and scoots the pitcher in my direction. "I missed you a lot, Steph. But I'm really fucking hurt."

An extra tear follows the stray I just wiped away. "I missed you, too. Maybe we can start up our girls' puzzle night again."

"Huh, right. Because Kris totally isn't ready to rip your head off, either."

My head droops in defeat. I grab the pitcher and shuffle back outside.

I just have to face it: I broke more than one relationship, and now I'm paying for it.

Maybe Ty was right when we were saying goodbye at Waffle House early this morning.

"You belong here," he murmured as his brown eyes

searched mine under a glaring light in the parking lot. It illuminated the red undertone of his curly brown hair swept to the side and allowed me to count the number of freckles dotting his nose and cheeks, made the half-inch gold plugs in his earlobes glint. "You belong at the studio."

His arms were firmly around my waist; every time I tried to finally get in my car, he would cinch me tighter and nuzzle my neck.

"Don't go. Move in with me."

I choke on a swallow of margarita, coughing enough to garner the attention of Mom and the twins sitting at the table.

I completely ignore the most tatted-up twin, whose black hair sits in a bun on top of his head, and head straight for the waterfall with my own personal pitcher of "sadaritas" in hand.

But the dim string lights overhead cast shadows over his tattooed arm with a gold watch and shiny rings adorning his fingers, emphasizing how much he's hit the gym.

My breath trembles on an exhale.

Hair raises on the back of my neck, and I meet Zak's gaze again.

I suck in an audible gasp before swallowing the ball of knives trying to make my throat bleed out.

"All this turned out really nice, Dad," I comment, unsure of where I should sit. I like facing everyone with my back to the wall. But I don't want to see them. But I don't trust to turn my back, either.

"Thanks," he says as he tosses aside a big weed he pulls from around the waterfall fixture. "Sure coulda used your help wrangling your mother in with—" he gestures widely, "—all this. But it's nice having this setup. Now she's talkin' about building a barn out back for weddings." He scoffs. "Like we don't got enough goin' on with NYB."

I feign a lighthearted chuckle. "Yeah. That keeps us busy almost year-round, anyway."

Dad gives a curt nod, picking another weed.

The margarita is delicious, but goddamn it, if the guilt that keeps rolling in doesn't coat my tongue in bitterness.

Before I left, his dark hair was a little salt and peppery. Now, it's more salt than pepper with only a few dark streaks left. He still wears his ratty Chucks, though, and a Black Sabbath T-shirt that he'll probably request to be buried in.

"I love you," I pipe up.

A glimmer of happiness finally appears on his face. "Love you, too, sweet pea. Really am glad to have you home." He gives the area one last sweep before stepping away. "I know Dave and Ty loved having you around, but I'm glad to have you back full time at the festival."

Deep down, I'll miss working at my dad's best friend's recording studio with my oldest childhood friend. But I'm excited to be back working full time at New Year's Ball calling the shots.

Dad slips away to join in on horseshoes as Brandy curls up in the corner and decides for me where I should sit. She's attentive to the game and ignores my presence, like she's sitting with me out of obligation and would rather be anywhere else but beside me.

I whip out my phone. It's around the time we would call it quits at the studio and meet up with a few musician friends for dinner and drinks at a food truck park.

Thin branches and twigs snap. Bushes rustle.

Shadows move in the corner of my eye.

The din of cicadas and crickets goes silent.

"Holy shit. Nobody move!"

Chapter 4

Buckout Road

–Concrete Dream

When Dad yells for everyone to stop in their tracks, you do as you're told. Especially when a black figure moves against the backdrop of dusky trees and shrubs.

The mixed stench of wet dog and musky horse announces its presence. Two tiny little dark lights glitter in the bushes, moving closer.

A black deer with a hell of a rack comes into view.

"Shit," Dad whispers. "The one time I don't have my damn gun out here…"

The deer stands completely still and watches us, as if it understands the threat. It doesn't even twitch an ear when something rustles in the bushes.

But nothing else follows—just the ever-present curtain of trees and bushes and cactus that obscures the shadows.

My stomach flips, bile nipping at the bottom of my throat.

The deer finally takes one step forward, as if testing to see if anyone will move. When no one does, it ambles off to the other side of the yard, pausing to bend its neck and sniff the grass. Gradually, it disappears into the trees.

A violent shiver rushes through me despite being at least ninety degrees out here.

"Gah, that was a gorgeous ten-pointer!" Dad exclaims breathlessly.

Brandy shakes her head, sinking further into her seat as she grips her glass of iced water tightly. "Somethin' wasn't right about that thing."

Robbie stares into the trees after the deer. His bearded face slowly sinks into a grimace, contorting in confusion. He shakes out of it a moment later, and when he notices me watching, he crosses his eyes and sticks out his pierced tongue.

Cicadas and crickets start singing again the second my chortle cuts through the silence.

"I better git to Kris and Drea," Shannon says. Footsteps sound behind me, and a boney arm wraps around my shoulders. "Come by and see the new place tomorrow. Our girl's been begging to see Abby."

I give his arm a reassuring squeeze, smiling at the memory of Drea completely forgoing any attempt at pronouncing "aunty" and calling me Abby, instead. "I'll be there."

Mom comes to the rescue, settling in beside me and asking Brandy about the upcoming photo shoot they have scheduled to update staff photos on the NYB website. Adrian approaches Dad and challenges him to a round of horseshoes, and Robbie responds by passive-aggressively tossing his shoes at Adrian's feet before plopping his heavy ass on my lap.

I heave. "Fuck, dude, lay off the beer and tacos!"

"Says the woman who can't say no to a waffle, apparently," he replies the same time he pinches the evidence of my Waffle House obsession.

I flick his nose where I saw blood. "Ugh!"

He yelps, immediately covering his nose and hightailing it until he's just out of arm's reach. "Missed you, too, shithead."

I grunt in response before tuning in to the horseshoes game. After Adrian makes his first toss, he glances at me and his mouth twists into that lopsided smirk I've known since Robbie proudly introduced us to his new bestie after religious ed.

Breath remains stuck in my chest, expecting Zak to appear. I freshen my drink, pounding back a chilly glassful in preparation until I give myself brain freeze.

But he never comes.

"C'mon, old man," Adrian jabs. "You still got a few good years left. Aim like you mean it!"

Dad barks a laugh. "Boy, I'll whoop your ass any day."

Peaking over my shoulder, the patio is empty.

Guess Zak hitched a ride with Shannon.

So I let myself settle into the overstuffed chair with my now not-so-sadarita.

Things aren't so bad. Not even when Adrian's face lights up a little more brightly when my smile turns into a simper.

But him kissing my hair before heading out leaves my stomach in a lurch that worsens with Brandy's glare thereafter.

After she gives Mom a hug and says goodnight, she spins around, ignoring my smile and readiness to hug her, too.

Robbie raises his brows. "I mighta gotten the beatdown tonight, but ouch."

I press my arms into my side to reassure myself. "Will you talk to her for me? She's practically my sister-in-law—she can't give me the cold shoulder forever."

"What's that? You want me to help *bail* you out of something?"

I focus on the starry sky above. I knew he'd mention

something about it. "Maybe you shouldn't beat the shit outta your best friends in public, asshat."

Brandy peeks around the corner of the house, practically sneering at me. "C'mon, Rob. I'm tired."

He throws an arm around my shoulders and squeezes. "Safe to say we're not best buds anymore." His mouth suddenly pinches into a tiny *O*. "Hey, just like you and Brandy. Look at us being twins."

I smack his shoulder as he walks away. "Not funny."

When I finally climb into bed, my eyes refuse to close.

Night consumes my room. The house creaks, settling in the wind, and mesquite scratches against siding. Fans in my and my parents' rooms blow on high and drown out cicadas. In my window, the occasional twinkle pokes through like phone lights in a crowd at a concert.

It makes me think of days I shouldn't be thinking of anymore because there's no way I can get them back.

Giving up, I get dressed and grab my phone. Ty responded with a selfie with our usual Friday night group squeezing in together for a group photo. They look like they're having plenty of fun, but Ty's message says something a little different.

> Wish you were here. Or I was there

> I miss you already

I know better than to send it, but I do, anyway.

> I miss you too

Ty's handsome face suddenly lights up on the screen, phone buzzing from his call.

Sighing heavily, my hand falls to the bed and I stare up at

the blank, dark ceiling. I suck in a sharp breath, flick my thumb, and bring the phone to my face. "Hey."

"Hey," he drags out in an excited tone. It doesn't cover up all the background noise of conversation, loud music, and people hollering. "Sorry, I know you hate phone calls. But I wanted to hear your voice."

"You heard it this morning," I remind him.

"Yeah, but it's not the same." He pauses. Ice clinks like it's right against the microphone. "Look, I'm serious: I'll fly out to San Antonio in a few weeks, if you want."

Someone in the background makes whipping sounds. "Ka-cha, ka-cha! Our boy's done for!"

Ty guffaws and I groan softly, rubbing my forehead.

Just what I need.

"Whatever," I say. "Just don't pick any fights when you visit, okay?"

"Hey, I'm a lover, not a fighter," he insists.

Guys and girls both hoot in the background.

I recognize a woman's voice, a singer I recorded recently. "Get it, Steph!"

I snort, grinning to myself. But the last time he visited while I was still with Zak is clear as day in my memory. "I'm serious. Let me get the temperature of the bullshit going on here and we'll figure something out if you just *have* to visit."

Ty almost chokes trying to get out, "I don't care what's going on. Just say the word and I'm there."

I have to smack the butterflies in my stomach with a figurative eighteenth century Bible. "We're just friends, Ty. Don't get your panties in a wad."

"Yeah," he affirms cheerfully, but I can still detect a hint of hurt. "Yeah, I know. But try telling our parents that."

I roll my eyes, suppressing a smile. Growing up, both our parents called us boyfriend and girlfriend—and I know that's why our friendship never sat well with Zak. "You know I will. Don't have too much fun without me."

"How can I? You were most of the fun, anyway."

When we hang up, I'm wide awake. So I get up, put on some loungewear, and grab my keys.

It's a bad habit I picked up before I left, driving around in the middle of bum fuck South Central Texas. But it's one that doesn't require me to be creative and forces me out of my head for a while, like being on high alert for deer and other critters crossing the road takes the focus off me being a shitty person long enough to put me in a better headspace for a couple of days.

At the end of our road, I take a left to head south. The road curves slightly, and behind that lies the bridge.

It's pitch black down there with the busted streetlight. Tall mesquite trees further obscure the view and create more shadows over the bridge.

The streetlight flickers, illuminating a figure standing on the edge of the bridge for a split second before going out again.

I suck in a sharp breath and grip the steering wheel tighter.

Turn your ass around right now.

But there is no turning around as the side of the road turns into patches of cactus, preventing me from flipping a quick U-ie.

The only way around is through and passing by the mystery person hanging out on the bridge.

The dark figure spins around, facing my direction as the car approaches.

God, please don't let it be la lechuza or the devil.

CHAPTER 5

WHO'S GOING HOME WITH YOU TONIGHT?

–TRAPT

YOU DUMB BITCH, THIS IS HOW GIRLS GET MURDERED IN HORROR MOVIES.

Drive faster so they can't catch you, dumbass!

But I drive on, anyway, keeping a close eye on the figure on the bridge.

They draw closer, becoming clearer.

Someone in dark clothes heads toward me. A few feet more, and the headlights shine on their face.

My heart drops into my stomach and forces the breath out of my lungs.

This is so much worse than a horror movie.

Zak blinks repeatedly, focusing on the car. Something isn't right with the way he stumbles.

Pulling up next to him, I roll my window down. "Zak? Are you okay?"

The streetlight flickers again, and recognition crosses his face. "Steph?"

"Yeah." I throw the car into park. "The hell are you doin' out here? Thought you got a ride from Shannon."

Zak trips forward, steadying himself on the car door

before lifting his head. He still has snake bite piercings and a ring in his nose on the opposite nostril from Adrian. His lips part, jaw unhinged in disbelief, and the bolt in his tongue twinkles in what little light there is around here. Every inch of visible skin except for his face is covered in tattoos.

The stench of liquor wafts into the car.

"Are you drunk?"

He averts his eyes, still supporting himself on the door. Even his fingers are covered in tattoos. "Um… sorry… Didn't know you were home."

I grumble under my breath, unsure of what I'm about to offer. But with the dive bar just a couple hundred yards away and his house a mile down the direction where I just came, I can connect the dots.

"Get in. I'll take you home."

Zak pushes away from the car so hard that he falls on his ass, grunting when he hits the asphalt. "Owee."

I stifle a chuckle as I climb out of the car. "C'mon, get in before you get cactus needles in your ass. *Really* don't wanna be the one to help you pull those out."

He scrambles away. "N-no."

Sighing, I ask, "Why?"

The streetlight flickers, and he looks over his shoulder at the approach, as if he heard something, searching until the light shutters off.

"Z, don't make this any more difficult than it already is," I beg. "Get in the car."

His attention lands on me again, studying me in the darkness.

He's not the sad, desperate guy I left behind. I mean, he's definitely sad the longer he stares at me, regardless of how inky black the air is between us.

But he's not the same.

This Zak is a man who's been working on himself, hitting

up the gym as much as the tattoo studio. He isn't the guy with a taco belly I fell head over heels for in high school.

But underneath the spiffed-up exterior, a flash of my high school sweetheart appears.

The corners of my lips twitch at the thought of my Chiquito without all the tattoos and muscles. He got all his piercings before graduating high school and had a lot of work done before I left, but with his knuckles, elbows, and neck now all filled in, it looks like he finally got all the painful parts done that he was avoiding.

Zak's expression falls, sinking like he recognizes something he wasn't prepared to see.

Like he sees his high school sweetheart, too.

Maybe he can still see the girl that had a plan for everything, the one that had a carefully laid-out twenty-year trajectory for Timeless to take over the world like Meshuggah or Gojira that he bought into wholeheartedly. The one that was his biggest fan.

Standing here in the middle of a midnight road, facing my past that was supposed to be my future, finally makes Atlanta disappear.

We both might have a lot to show for the past year and a half—tattoos and muscles and an album for him, an extra fifteen pounds and so many tracks produced for me—but the fight earlier and the tension between us says it all.

Neither of us have done any better since I've been gone.

Acid gnaws at my heart.

Or maybe it's the goddamn guilt renewed all over again.

A whining buzz in my ears shakes me out of it to offer him a hand. "Come on. Let's get outta here before we get eaten alive by these damn mosquitoes."

He shakes his head. "No."

Groaning, I tell him, "You've had too much to drink. You can't walk home."

"Ha, watch me."

Rolling my eyes, I grab his brawny arm, anyway, and pull him up. He careens forward too quickly and sends me stumbling back into the car.

Jesus Christ, he's got abs now?

I try pushing Zak away as I peek over his shoulder, into the trees and over the abandoned approach, wondering if the owl is still there.

My skin crawls.

Zak's stare is both fiery and icy. His body heat is unmistakable from the Texas swelter, even with the gentle breeze that doesn't do shit except make stifling South Texas air swirl and choke lungs.

A familiar feeling stirs deep in my stomach with his body still pressed to mine.

"What're you doin' here?" Zak asks with furrowed brows.

I nudge his hips to give him a hint. "Didn't you hear? I'm the creative director at NYB now."

The streetlight flashes and glints off his golden frames.

"Those glasses make you look like a douchebag, by the way."

He chuckles, gaze softening. His hands cradle my face and thumbs graze my cheeks, and his lips part like he's about to say something, but nothing comes out.

"Y-y—you're...," he finally stutters. His eyes close and he bites his lip. He shakes his head slightly before taking a deep breath. "You're a lot prettier than I remember."

The way he gazes down at me with hitched breath as frogs and crickets sing their chorus around us sends me all the way back to high school, back to when he pulled me aside after our first gig post-label signing and kissed me for the first time.

The way he trembled that night resonates in his fingers touching my face now.

All of it makes my eyes burn. Especially when I glance at his mouth so close now.

I push him away, grab his hands, and lead him to the passenger side of the car. "Alcohol will do that."

Zak doesn't say anything else as I usher him into the passenger seat and shut the door.

Turning to face the approach, I survey the area shrouded in shadow and night, trying to discern any creature of the night. Still nothing out here except a truck leaving the bar and heading the other direction.

The ride is silent beyond the screaming music playing at a low volume. I don't offer anything, and neither does Zak as I pull into a driveway to turn around and head north, just a half mile past my road.

Suppose misery loves company, but, fuck—*really?*

The Ramos estate is exactly as I left it beyond the tree line hiding a Spanish revival style house from the road. It spans wide with a clay-tiled roof and beige stucco walls, and the heavy wooden front door glows in golden light within a hidden archway. Behind the house lies a pool and a small building that hosts Timeless's headquarters, and beyond that are acres of land for cattle.

A new deep purple Hellcat and blue Tacoma replaces Zak's Cutlass and Adrian's Suburban in the roundabout driveway. I pull up to the front door around a live oak tree and park, glancing between the new rides and the house I used to hang out at almost every single day for seven years.

Cutting the engine, music roars through the stucco. Lucky for Adrian they live without neighbors nearby so he can make as much noise as he wants.

Zak leans against the window, softly snoring. I bite back the urge to push stray locks of hair out of his face and shake his shoulder, instead. "Hey, wake up. We're home."

I wince at that last part.

Gradually, he rouses, looking around with closed eyes. "Huh?"

I grumble all the way to the passenger door and growl as I attempt to pull him out of my car. When he finally emerges, his bodyweight propels him forward. I almost trip over myself gaining footing as I shove him back against the car—he must've gained at least fifty pounds of muscle, he's so fucking heavy.

"C'mon," I grunt as I slip an arm around his waist and pull his arm over my shoulders.

Dragging him to the front door is like pulling a freight train.

I jiggle the knob. Locked.

"Z, where're your keys?"

"Mm?"

"Goddamn it," I whisper, trying to keep his heavy arm around me as I hold him upright and search his pockets. Unfortunately, that means my forehead pressing into the crook of his neck so I can reach around him.

The bitch giggles, grinning as his head tilts back. "Oh, this is fun."

"Shut up, ass."

The scent of alcohol and sweat fills my nostrils as I hunt through his pockets. My finger loops through a metal key ring, but I linger.

When Zak's arm slips from my shoulders, down across my back, and his hand rests on my hip, everything in my body seizes.

I *really* shouldn't be hugging Zak like this, missing the way he feels in my arms, the scorch of his body on mine, the rhythm of his heartbeat under my touch...

His mouth is *right. There.*

"Mm, babe?" he mumbles, tilting his head toward me.

Chapter 6

Pull Me Under

–Dream Theater

I COULD TAKE ADVANTAGE OF THIS SITUATION.

I could press my mouth to Zak's and kiss him for the first time in nearly two years. Proceed to vomit out all the apologies I've rehearsed over and over in my head until I gave myself a migraine.

I'd probably get away with it, too, because a sad drunk brain is a desperate one.

Or maybe he'd push me away, ask what the fuck is wrong with me, and tell me to go home. To stay away.

Even worse, he's probably tried to drink the memory of seeing me away so he wouldn't remember anything I say or do, anyway.

It's so slight, but the coolness of Zak's lip piercings tingle on my forehead.

My skin literally peels when I force myself to tear away.

I can't do that to him. No matter how much I want him to forgive me, I don't deserve it.

I push the door a little too hard and it bangs against the wall like a gunshot.

A shirtless Adrian jumps up from the leather sectional in the great room just ahead. An obnoxious vape cloud swirls around that he waves off with a book. "The fuck?"

I kick the door shut behind us and start leading Zak to the right, toward the hallway where his bedroom is. "Little help would be nice!"

Adrian tosses the book aside. "Yeah, yeah. I got him," he responds, grabbing Zak's arm to throw over his shoulders.

But he doesn't take him down the hallway to the right—he leads Zak to the left, disappearing into the darkness of the hallway that leads toward what used to be Kris's, Shannon's, and their daughter's rooms. Before that, it was their parents' side of the house.

I hang back between the foyer and great room, watching the twins until they disappear. It's bad enough I'm here in their house—I really don't want to follow to make sure Zak gets into bed okay.

Dream Theater blaring through the sound system scrambles my thoughts. I peek over the back of the couch, finding the remote beside Adrian's book.

He's read *The Hellbound Heart* so many times that I stopped counting. When I flip the cover open, dates line the inside in different colored inks, sometimes smudged pencil. I recognize some as tour dates.

I snort, tossing the book and remote back onto the couch after turning the music down. "Nerd."

"Uh, sorry about that."

I jump, staring wide eyed at Adrian approaching from the hallway.

"I thought he hitched a ride with Shannon."

"Yeah," I respond. "So did I."

Neither of us say another word, studying each other in this house so familiar, yet foreign.

Adrian's gaze makes me want to scratch and peel until my fingers are bloody and my skin flakes off—anything to make him stop staring at me the way he is right now, like he's absorbing as much of my presence as he can before I disappear into thin air.

"I'll get out of your hair."

"Hey, no," he says, stepping in my way. "Stay 'n' hang out for a bit."

I really shouldn't.

But the longer my stare lingers on Adrian, the more pronounced his lopsided smile becomes and the more my flesh crackles beneath my skin.

He nods toward the great room. "Have a seat. I'll grab some beer."

Adrian heads for the kitchen, and I glimpse at the door arguing with me to get the hell out.

But Adrian reappears with a couple of beers and hands me one. "Thanks for pickin' him up. Bet he woulda woken up with West Nile in the morning if you didn't."

I take a reluctant swig before nodding. "Yeah, probably."

He throws an arm around my shoulders, probably as insurance against me running away, and leads me past a couple of guitars in stands along the wall. He snags his vape rig from the coffee table before settling into the leather couch beside me.

"How was Atlanta?" he asks. "You never text back or post anything online, so I don't know what's been goin' on."

"The studio kept me busy."

He blows a gigantic cloud of white vapor into the living room. Smells like cookies and skunk. "Too busy to answer the phone unless it was Shannon or Rob?"

"Sounds about right."

Adrian taps his fingertips against the book sitting on the cushion between us. The silence is marked by epic vocals and wailing riffs at a low volume, and a peculiar tension grips my stomach.

"Was it the studio, or Ty?"

"Tsk, fuck's it to you, dude?"

He snorts. "Good to know that attitude hasn't changed."

I roll my eyes, cross an arm over my stomach, and take an extra large gulp of beer. Him and Zak both have always made their opinion on Ty known, but I don't give a shit—Ty's been around a hell of a lot longer than they have.

"So," Adrian starts after another hit from his vape, "surprised I never heard anything about you joining a new band."

"Left my guitars here," I respond curtly.

"Uh-huh. You mean to tell me the notorious Stephani Wade hasn't picked up guitar since she quit Timeless?"

"I didn't see a point in playing anymore."

"Why?" he asks, turning to face me after blowing more vapor. His terra-cotta skin glows, probably from spending every free moment on tour soaking up the sun poolside or floating the river.

I miss tubing.

"That's what you do: you're a guitarist." A tiny simper brightens his face. "You're the Petrucci to my Portnoy, princesa."

"Ha, you're good, but don't compare yourself to Portnoy, hon."

Adrian slaps his hand over his heart as if he were wounded.

I wish I could say I hate sharing a laugh with him.

I lean my arm against the back of the couch and rest my head in my hand, searching the house beyond Adrian and drinking the cold cerveza. My curiosity is piqued by the notebooks full of lyrics and musical notations scattered over every available surface.

"I see that look, Steph."

My gaze snaps back to Adrian. "What look?"

His eyes glimmer as he watches me. "You miss it."

"What?"

Adrian throws his chin toward the guitars. "Playing."

I stare long and hard at the guitars and ideas and plans, remembering what it was like hanging out here all the time, rehearsing and screwing around on the guitar until a single riff set off a bar that turned into a whole song. Like our brain waves aligned perfectly with the universe to translate its message into something personal with words and sounds that would one day speak to someone through their earbuds or speakers. Then, one day, that same someone would come to a Timeless gig to worship us playing our hearts out on stage, resurrecting the universe's message right before people's eyes over and over and over—

"I see it, alright," Adrian interrupts.

I recognize the look on his face: admiration.

Adrian holds his vape to my lips, beckoning them to part. I cover his hand with mine, taking the rig from him, and breathe in.

He rises from the couch and ambles toward the guitars. I can't stop staring at the way his red gym shorts cling to an ass you could sink some serious teeth into.

When he turns around, I quickly refocus on Zak's acoustic in his hand.

"So what was that fight about earlier?"

Adrian sits beside me, pausing before holding the guitar toward me. "Play something and I'll tell you."

I glower at him. "I'm not playing anything."

He shrugs, starting to pluck the strings. "Guess you don't wanna know, then."

"Brandy said y'all have been fighting almost nonstop."

He nods. "Yeah."

"About what?"

He stops fiddling, but he holds it out to me again. "You show, and I'll tell."

I'm certain my eyes have turned into molten stone on him.

Polishing off my beer and handing him the empty bottle, I tell him, "Get me another."

I help myself to a couple more hits from his vape, studying the guitar across my lap. Funny that this is the Gibson Zak would lend me back in the day.

Adrian finds me lightly dragging my finger down the strings.

"Eventually you're gonna have to quit the foreplay and do the damn thing."

"Oh, hush."

I chug at least half the beer before situating the guitar on my lap the right way, staring down the spruce neck like it's a diabolical device.

Adrian's stare claws at my skin, finagling beneath the epidermis and burrowing deep into pores and capillaries, but I ignore it. Right now, I'm cradling my past over my lap and in my hands. It surrounds me in this very room.

Maybe I should just let some things die. I should let everything in this house go.

The guitar suddenly weighs like a thousand suns, burning my hands. I set it aside, placing it on the couch between us before getting up.

"Where're you goin'?"

"I shouldn't be here."

Footsteps follow, and a hand grabs mine, forcing me to come face to face with Adrian.

"Things were so much better when you were in the band," he admits. "Nothing's been the same since you left. Timeless fuckin' sucks without you."

I snatch my hand from his. "That's not my problem

anymore."

The door is right there, demanding my exit.

Adrian suddenly spins me around and pushes me against it.

His hands cup my face as he presses his lips to mine.

Chapter 7

Bad Habits

—Ed Sheeran ft. Bring Me The Horizon

IT'S THE LITTLE THINGS THAT MAKE THE BIGGEST impact, right? Just that one little mistake after another that tumbles down what looks like a gentle slope but is actually a mountain, all of it melding into one big, gigantic mistake.

The kind that upends lives, ruins hopes and dreams.

Adrian parts slightly. The scent of vape juice and Mexican beer lingers on his breath passing over my lips. "You shouldn't have left."

The pad of his thumb brushes over my bottom lip, forcing me to finally look.

His eyes are wide and dark, hypnotized as he leans down.

I pull away, but his fingers tangle in my hair and force me to turn so his mouth catches mine.

Adrian's touch is dangerous. Delicious.

Familiar.

I wish I could say I'm turning away, telling him no, and storming out to head back home, or at the very least camp in my car since it feels like my brain is vacating my head.

But he remembers exactly where to touch me.

One hand seizes my hip, pressing me against the door as the other circles my throat. His mouth follows from the edge of mine, up my jawline, down my neck.

Thank fuck I finally push him away.

"I don't wanna do this again."

He traces my collarbone before venturing further and brushing along the neckline of my shirt, down the sensitive skin on top of my breasts. He bends to my ear and murmurs, "Things are different," before his teeth graze the lobe.

It's hard to breathe with my heart hammering against my sternum and Adrian tilting my head, allowing him to easily taste my neck.

Sucking in a sharp breath, I pull him closer.

Adrian lifts me up by the ass. I cling to his shoulders, and he hooks my legs around his waist.

Our mouths locked tight don't give me any chance in hell.

Things are different with Adrian's room now in Zak's old, expanded room.

Adrian tosses me onto the bed and crawls over me. Drumstick calluses on his hands threaten to kindle a long-buried flame as they scrape over the tender flesh of my hips and stomach.

My inner walls throb, aching from forcing myself to stay still, to fight the urge to go any further.

I gasp when his dick hardens between my legs wrapped around him. My hips automatically grind up, eager to accommodate his girth, and my teeth sink into his bottom lip.

Adrian's soft groan radiates goosebumps all over my skin.

Clothes are fucking constricting. I shed my shirt and bra, tossing them into the darkness of this room consuming us both.

Dim lamp light reveals Adrian's stupor before he drops down to kiss my chest. Humid pecks make my nipples prick, and a wave of wetness rushes through my core, especially when he nips and licks the hardened buds.

I fucking hate that a whine slips from my throat. I bite down hard on my bottom lip, a reminder to get a hold of myself.

Adrian's tongue traces the longhorn skull dripping with coral honeysuckle and spider lilies tattooed across my sternum and ribs. He moans softly, as if the honeysuckle on my skin tastes as sweet as the real thing. "This is new."

I lift his chin to make him look up at me. Gently, I trace the nose piercing he's had since he graduated high school and got the same time Zak and Robbie got theirs done. A bar in his left nipple glints, and I gently flick it. He gives a small yelp, uselessly covering his pec and frowning at me.

Snorting, I say, "So is this."

My fingertips trace the lines of black script, gray shading, and negative space spanning from shoulder to shoulder announcing El Diablo.

"You're the devil, huh? Makes a lot of sense."

He chortles under his breath as his hands come up to my breasts. I follow the outlines of the smashed and broken clock tattooed on one hand and the hellhound stamped on the other.

He kisses upward from my sternum. "You wouldn't believe me if I told you."

I laugh a little more loudly, the sound laden with bitterness. "I'd believe it."

Adrian hovers over my mouth. His heart thrums against my chest like it's trying to beat mine into submission. "I didn't make you do anything you didn't already want to."

Anger boils in my belly, threatening to burst and send Adrian flying into the ceiling so I can find my clothes and leave, never to look back at the Ramos estate, home, San Antonio, any of this.

I didn't come back just to be taunted for something I can't make amends over or succumb to the very same temptation that fucked everything up.

But my body is heavy, and the sheets grip my limbs and refuse to let me leave this bed.

Shadowy fog lifts my brain in my skull, snapping the connection to any sense I have left and sends me all the way to the back of Adrian's Suburban, where I thought he had passed out from all the liquor and weed at a bonfire, but his arm wrapped around my ribs and held me tight, and my head turned, and our lips brushed, and his hands searched until they were groping my breast and slinking into my underwear, and—

His lips sweep over my mouth, teasing a kiss that doesn't come to fruition, and he rocks ever so slightly to make his rock-hard cock rub against my clit.

"I hate you," I groan as his hips crush mine, just like before.

Adrian's fingers yank my hair, tearing me away from his sultry mouth. Darkness overshadows half his face, reminding me of the place I'm quickly backsliding into, warning me that it's not too late to turn back, to tell him to go fuck himself and go to hell.

"Then fuck me like you hate me."

His tongue slips over mine, making his case for me to stay right where I am. I command my fingers to yank his hair back.

All they do is weld our mouths together.

His hips roll. My nails sink into his shoulders. He inhales sharply before pushing away to rip off my shorts and panties.

Those darkened eyes feast on my figure, the sight of the devil in my life cannibalizing me beneath him and paring me down to bare bones with a glowing scrutiny that threatens total combustion.

His tattooed hand slips beneath the elastic waistband of his shorts, and he strokes himself. His breath quivers on an exhale.

My inner walls clench, and my head spins.

When I blink, his shorts are down around his thighs and I'm the one stroking his length.

Adrian tips my chin upward and kisses me.

God fucking damn it.

"Get a condom."

The more things change, the more things stay the same.

I want to stop kissing him. I want to push Adrian away. I don't want to be in his bed. Especially not tonight.

But I'm here.

My lips are locked onto his. I'm pulling him closer, whining as his body heat sets my flesh ablaze.

My head swims, eyes threatening to roll to the back of my head from Adrian's touch alone with his mouth on mine and fingers swirling over my clit.

"Fuck me," I whisper, voice drifting away from me. "Please, fuck me."

Warmth floods my pussy as he positions himself with a shaking breath. We groan in unison as he fills me with slow, measured thrusts.

"Could you get any wetter?" Adrian chuckles breathily. His lips tremble on mine. "Fuck…"

"Shut up," I mutter, forcing my mouth onto his. My nails claw into his back and I whimper when he plunges just right.

I hate how he settles inside me, like being buried so deeply in my pussy searing from the ache of needing him is exactly where he belongs.

He sighs my name softly in my ear before his lips trail down my throat, voice husky on my neck. "I missed this."

His hot breath singes, an invisible masterpiece canvassing over my skin—a private, custom piece only for me to admire in memory later, where I, one hundred and ten percent, definitely will not be touching myself.

He moans loudly in pure rapture.

My eyes roll back.

"I missed you."

Shoving his shoulder, I wrestle my way on top, resting my hands on his tattooed chest and sinking onto his erect cock. Resisting the moan building deep within my chest transforms it into a loud cry when pleasure coaxes me to let go.

I hate the way his hands clutch my hips, the way his fingers dig into my flesh. I hate the way he groans through gritted teeth. I hate the way his eyes eat me alive.

I hate how it all makes me ride him harder.

He's barely audible above the bed creaking and slamming rhythmically against the wall. "Fuck, baby. Just like that."

It's automatic: I slap Adrian across the face.

He glares at me, and my hand circles his throat, pressing down.

"I fucking hate you," I utter through a clenched jaw, glowering back at him.

Adrian swallows hard, his throat bobbing underneath. His hips lift and force mine further down, making us grind together like a screeching train wreck on rails that can't be stopped.

His eyes flutter as he forces me to take him all the way.

I hate how he makes my pussy sing for him.

With my hand still around his throat, I slap him again. His eyes pop wide open, and I spit on his face.

"You're a piece of *shit*."

Adrian's eyes glaze over. The spit trickles down his cheek, just like his hand slipping from my hip. His thumb presses against my clit and begins to tease.

"Yeah?" he breathes. "Fuck're you gonna do about it?"

The whimper that falls out of me is high-pitched. Desperate. Pleading.

I slap him again and again and again, his skin stinging my palm and groans filling the darkness.

He captures my clit just right, sending fire blazing up my core and through my spine.

The way my hips rock and roll is reckless and rough as I cinch Adrian's throat even tighter. His throat vibrates against my palm in a steady, on-going moan. My pussy tightens watching his eyes flutter, hearing his moans soften, his breath weakening under my firm grip.

I could scream from the tension of being in Adrian's bed, the friction from fucking him so roughly threatening to send me flying when I don't even want to be here.

But the point of no return never existed, and I'm so close.

A frustrated growl resonates from deep within my chest as I let go to grip the bed. Adrian heaves, and his fingers bury deep into pelvic bone and press harder against my clit.

The bed hammers out its own solo to the sway of my hips over his, and his moans soar to ecstatic heights.

"Shit," Adrian gasps, hips bucking.

Lightning surges through my clit, and I scream from the sudden explosion consuming the barren field of my life, cleared by my attempt to start over fresh from the worst mistake I've made. The flames gorge themselves on the remaining vermin of animosity, disgust, and contempt that demolished the good I had and made me leave everything behind.

Bringing me right back to what started it all.

I collapse on the bed. Breathless. Head spiraling. Legs trembling and pussy throbbing. A whine slips when my clit pulses from a lingering shock.

Adrian pants, almost wheezing. "Jesus *fucking* Christ."

My eyelids fall, letting the darkness consume me.

The barren field in my mind is dark and cold, spinning way too fast for me to make heads or tails of which way is up and which way is down.

But my body warms with someone next to me, anchoring my twisty world to a familiar demon.

Knots form at the back of my head. They force my mouth onto something soft and damp.

My lips part and my tongue runs over another, moaning softly when sweltering heat parts my legs. The heat wave sweeps over my sensitive clit and elicits a whine from me.

I yelp when my pussy is smacked hard, the sound disgustingly wet like a soaking swimsuit fresh out of the river dropping onto a tile floor.

A shadowy figure with a gravelly voice rumbles so close to my ear but from so far away. "I'm not done with you yet."

My legs shake. My breath quakes.

White-hot lightning zings through my core and I cry out, clinging to the blistering form beside me.

Lips move against mine. "Tell me you're my whore."

I scream when a hand claps right against my clit, so loud that it echoes and rings in my ears in the vast emptiness.

Fingers cut off oxygen and make me focus on the face in front of mine.

Haziness of the high obscures features, but I recognize Adrian by the taste of him on my tongue, like a mangonada sweetened by sin, tangy and tart with regret, and spiced up to eleven by hatred and desire.

He's the devil destroying everything with fire and flame, a grand holocaust that annihilates another life to reveal the old one I left behind still there, lying in wait for me to pick up almost exactly where I left off.

"Tell me you're my whore, or I will fuck your throat till

you pass out." He sucks in a shaky breath, exhaling on the smallest moan. "I'll make you choke on my come."

His palm stings my pussy again, and I howl.

The vast, freezing emptiness of the field transforms into the fiery pit of hell, burning me alive with Adrian by my side.

"*Yes.*"

Chapter 8

The River

—Wage War

A BRIGHT LIGHT MAKES ME GROAN AND TURN AWAY from the source to hide. The scent of coffee hits my nose, and my eyes crack open.

I bolt upright when I realize I'm not in my apartment in Atlanta. I'm not in my room at my parents'.

I'm naked, in Adrian's bed, at the twins' place.

Groaning softly, I scrub a hand over my face before falling back and staring at the blank ceiling. My brain is firmly in place, reminding me how much I've already fucked up less than twenty-four hours after arriving home. I guess if I fucked up again, waking up in a bed is a lot more comfortable than the back of a Suburban.

I have to pry myself from Adrian's pillowy-soft bed after rubbing the sleep out of my eyes. Gradually, I shuffle over to the window and peep outside.

The Hellcat and Tacoma are both in the driveway.

Fuck.

Maybe I can sneak away without either of the twins noticing.

Yanking my clothes back on, I take a quick glance around

Adrian's new room that's huge and completely different from his teen boy room. The walls are devoid of band posters and painted a bright white, and a lapis lazuli bedspread adds color to the room's Spanish revival style that matches the rest of the house. Black walnut built-ins span the complete length of the far wall, stuffed to the gills with books—way more than he had before I left.

Black candles dot the shelves with a couple of saint statues, a single black rosary, and an assortment of knick-knacks. Picking one up to examine more closely, my eyes widen and I suddenly drop it.

Teeth and bones.

I have to shake off the shock.

The Ramos family owns a popular botanica in the city—they're brujas y brujos, and sometimes their work goes into dark places. I just remember Adrian always thumbing his nose at it, thinking brujeria and the Catholic faith he was raised in both were hokey. Maybe he's changed his mind about it and gotten into the darker side of things with dried blood on some of the remains.

Wiping my hands on my shorts, I crack the bedroom door open just enough to check for movement. Gradually, I creep down the hall, all the while keeping an eye on the other end of the house to make sure Zak doesn't suddenly appear.

Someone's in the kitchen opening and shutting cabinets.

Back pressed against the wall, I take a deep breath before cautiously peeking around the corner.

The Ramos twin in the kitchen has short hair and not so many tattoos.

When his back is turned, I leap across the doorway to hide behind the other wall so Adrian can't see me. My core muscles tremor as I peek around another corner into the great room to make sure Zak isn't hanging out in there.

All clear.

I slip out of hiding and make a dash for the front door.

"Ay, princesa. No need to duck and run."

I stop in my tracks, spinning around to find Adrian eyeballing me from the hallway I just came with a steaming mug at his lips. He's shirtless, fully showing off the tattoos adorning his upper half and his nipple piercing. His gym shorts cling to hips that dip into a deliciously soft V pointing south.

My eyes meet Adrian's again, and his brow quirks. "Zak's still passed out."

Okay, *now* I can breathe.

"You want coffee?"

I clear my throat. "Ah… maybe not. Thanks."

He draws closer. "Okay."

We stare at each other for an uncomfortably long moment before I start to back away, jabbing my thumb over my shoulder. "I really should be going."

Adrian steps forward and grabs my jaw before I have the chance to run, planting his mouth squarely on mine.

White-hot flashes pulse through my body, and memories of last night linger behind closed eyelids. Not of images, but of sensations and moans, of Adrian making me come over and over, torturing me until I couldn't even groan or whisper his name.

My thighs rub together when memories of coming so hard, so much sting. My clit electrifies, and my pussy throbs. I know he hears me whimper softly.

When he finally pulls away and I start breathing again, he studies my face in a way that feels far too intimate for the morning after a rough hate-fuck.

"Really wish you'd stick around," Adrian finally murmurs, hand firmly cradling my jaw. His black hair is disheveled, like he got up not too long ago and has run his hands through it repeatedly. "Even the house hasn't felt the same with you gone."

I shake his grip loose and step back. "It's your fault I left."

Adrian's jaw clenches. "You shoulda stayed. We could've figured things out."

A pained scoff blows past my lips. "What the fuck was there to figure out, huh?"

Adrian follows, footsteps rushing behind. "Stephani, wait."

I don't. I head straight for the door and fling it wide open.

I flinch the same time a girl jumps in front of me, staring with wide blue eyes under dark bangs.

She blinks, regaining composure as she gathers that I'm not one of the twins. Then, recognition lights up her eyes. "Holy shit, Stephani Wade?"

"Uh, yeah," I confirm unsurely.

She glances between me and the body drawing closer behind me. "Are you back in the band?"

I swallow the lump forming in my throat. "No."

"Dang," she pouts pitifully. "I thought it was a lot cooler when Timeless had some estrogen."

"Yeah," Adrian agrees. "So did I."

Her expression turns curious. "So… you're back with Zak, then?"

That question shouldn't send blood rushing through my veins in a boiling rage. "Sorry, who are you?"

"Oh, my bad! Guess I should introduce myself." She shoves her hand toward me with a smile. "I'm Norma. Adrian's girlfriend."

Fucking PLAY IT COOL, STEPHANI.

I tamp down the shock so it doesn't reveal itself on my face when my heart plummets all the way to my ass and threatens to upchuck right onto *Adrian's girlfriend's* feet.

It's covered up, instead, by mimicking her as I reach out to shake her hand. "Nice to meet you."

Don't fucking look at him.

"Well, sorry to cut things short, but I really gotta git."

I slip past her and all but run to my car, sucking in the shakiest breath when I dare to steal a glance at the front door.

Norma leans in to kiss Adrian, and he quickly angles to where she lands on his cheek instead of his mouth. She waltzes through the front door like she's been here a million times before.

My brows furrow when a pang plummets through my stomach.

His dark eyes sharpen on me, staring far too intently. The only thing that breaks it is my phone buzzing in the cupholder.

A slew of texts and missed phone calls clutter the screen over Mom calling me.

"Hey, hi, I'm *so* sorry—"

"Where the hell are you?" Mom shrieks. "We've been calling and texting and you haven't answered at all!"

"I-I'm sorry. I forgot my phone in the car."

"Where are you?"

I peer up, and the front door is closed. "I'm at the twins'."

Silence.

A very long moment of silence.

"I went out for a drive to clear my head and found Zak walking home from the bar," I explain. "He had too much to drink. Figured I'd get him home safe. Ended up passing out here."

More silence.

"Mom?"

"Are you and Zak working things out?"

I make a face. "What? I just said he was drunk. We talked

long enough for me to get him into the car. He was passed out by the time we got here. "

Mom huffs. "Well, glad to know you're not dead in a ditch somewhere or haven't run off, at least."

"I'm heading your way now. Promise."

I toss my phone aside and let my head fall back into the headrest. My head bangs against it repeatedly as I bitch at myself for doing this, for letting Adrian get to me *again*.

It's been a year and a half, a whole other goddamn city and state, and Adrian puts me back in a chokehold my very first night back home.

Literally and figuratively.

My eyes close in defeat. Now, I fucked someone else's boyfriend, and I'm the other woman.

When I drive away from the Hellcat and Tacoma, jealousy roils in my stomach. It weighs on the edge of my mind, too, that someone remembers me from the original lineup.

I don't want to make a comeback, I lie to myself as I take a right onto the road heading south. I can't make a comeback.

But if I had stayed in Timeless, I could be surrounded by guitars in my own home studio. I could be the one with all the notebooks full of ideas and inspiration leading to the next Timeless album.

And maybe Timeless wouldn't be in the middle of the total shit show they're in now.

"Not your problem," I grumble as my fingers drum against the steering wheel.

Besides, Adrian wanted me to stay and work things out? I don't know how anything could've worked out after we hooked up.

Not after Zak proposed.

They're *twin brothers*, for fuck's sake.

The glint of a familiar vehicle on the side of the road

heading toward the bridge catches my attention. I pass by the road home and park behind Brandy's red Camry, sure to leave plenty of space between my tires and sharp cactus needles before climbing out.

She's looking up into the trees with fists on her hips. Her bright auburn hair glowing in the morning sun and spray tan hiding the Gondor beacon glow is unmistakable.

"Hey," I call out.

She jumps and spins around, staring at me with wide eyes before breathing a sigh of relief. "Scared the freakin' shit outta me."

"Sorry. What're you doin'?"

Brandy glances at the approach and points at it. "I think there's something up there."

"Oh, no," I say, voice lowered an octave. "Hell no. It's probably that damn owl I saw last night. I wouldn't go up there."

She frowns, chewing the inside of her lip.

"I saw Gigi at the store last night," I mention. "She said there's been high schoolers doin' their bullshit here again, leaving offerings. Bet it's just something like that."

"Gigi, huh?" Brandy says with a small smirk. But it falls as quickly as it showed. "You said you saw an owl?"

I groan. "C'mon, Brandy, don't tell me you think it's la lechuza." I perk up. "On second thought, please do. Then that really means we shouldn't go pokin' around up there."

She snatches my hand and starts dragging me to the other side of the road and toward the overgrowth of trees, brush, and mustang grapevines. "You're comin' with me whether you like it or not."

CHAPTER 9

SPLINTER CELL

–Darko

My visceral reaction is to snatch my hand from Brandy and run away because fuck that owl and everything with it—I ain't about to fuck around and find out if it is la lechuza.

But the grip she has around my hand is vice-like and impossible to escape.

"I swear to fuckin' God," I start as she drags me through prickly trees and dodges random patches of cactus. Clouds overhead darken. "If I get bit by a rattlesnake or cursed from stickin' my nose where it don't belong, I'm gonna haunt your ass *forever*. You hear me?"

Brandy snorts, hopping a wire panel fence and waiting for me to follow. "At least then I know you won't leave me."

I land on the other side with a grunt, choosing not to smart back with anything.

During the spring and early summer, vegetation normally blocks the view and the way to the abandoned approach. But, being in the dog days of August, everything is brown, fried, crispy, and dead beneath the Texas sun.

Thorny mesquite scrapes my arms and legs, stinging as

they leave behind cuts and welts on my sandy beige skin. I catch a trickle of blood until I run into Brandy's back.

She gasps, eyes wide and horrified, as she clamps a hand over her mouth. "Oh, my God."

My nose wrinkles at the coppery smell, and I have to look away.

A black ten-point deer lays sawed in half on the approach. Entrails spill out from between its ribs, where blood has gushed out and dried over a chalk pentagram. A bottle of whiskey sits before the deer's open cavity, and puddles of hardened black wax mark each point of the pentagram.

Bloody shoe prints fade past us like a grisly ghost leaving the scene.

A fresh, hot wave of sweet and musty copper hits me with a force so hard that I stumble backwards, lightheaded.

Gigi wasn't lying: someone's been coming to the bridge and leaving offerings. But I don't think she was talking about a formal ritual sacrifice.

This isn't even the right goddamn bridge—the Devil's Bridge of Losoya is hidden deep in the woods over the creek not too far from my parents'.

Brandy holds her hands to her stomach, gagging. "I'm gonna be sick."

A blood-curdling screech sounds from right above us.

We both yelp and bolt away from the bloody deer.

We might be right over the river, but the blood rushing through my ears and the both of us gasping as we cower behind a measly mesquite is far louder as I peek around the thin limbs of the tree.

The wind is knocked out of me, and not out of relief.

I recognize that goddamn owl in the fucking tree above the deer, staring directly at us with big, pitch black eyes.

"Jesus Christ, that thing is so much bigger than I thought it was," I whisper. It has to be at least the size of Brandy.

"Are they supposed to be out during the day?" Brandy furiously whispers back, so low that I can hardly hear her.

I respond as quietly as I possibly can. "They come out during the day."

The owl flaps its gigantic white wings and swoops down, kicking up dust before landing right next to the sacrificed deer. It shifts and shudders, inspecting the gruesome display.

Its ivory beak flushes red as it pokes and prods at guts, yanking bloody intestines out before feasting.

The morning sun stops beating down on the approach as dark clouds loom overhead.

I grab Brandy's hand and yank her back. "Nope, nope, nope," I repeat under my breath, rushing us back down the gentle slope to get the fuck away.

Nothing else is said until after we jump the fence and slowly approach our cars.

Brandy gradually comes to a complete stop and bends over, heaving.

Her hair is already pulled back in a ponytail, but I reach over to pat her back. She can't even handle on-screen animal deaths—this will definitely scar her for life.

"What the *fuck* was that?" Brandy finally shouts, tears welling in her big doe eyes. "Something's not right with that thing!"

I grimace, watching her straighten up. "I told you it was a bad idea to go up there."

Brandy gasps for air, wiping the back of her hand across a sweaty forehead. She's shaking.

"Think you can make it home?"

She nods, taking a few more deep breaths. Finally, she asks, "What do we do? Who the fuck do you call for something like this?"

"Would a Ghostbusters reference be in poor taste right now?"

Groaning, she rolls her eyes and slaps my arm. "That's not even funny."

"Everyone knows to keep an eye out on the bridge," I offer. "Weird stuff happens once in a while. This isn't exactly out of the ordinary."

"It's just... it's so scary. Who does that? Who butchers an innocent animal like that?" Her button nose wrinkles. "And what kind of owl eats dead deer in the daylight?"

Grimacing, I look around at the dead mesquite trees beneath a now bluish-gray sky, wondering what—*who*—the fuck is out there.

"Someone in serious need of therapy," I respond. "And an owl that's probably sick."

Or something that's not exactly an owl.

Brandy glances over her shoulder in the direction of the approach, shivering violently despite the heat already sweltering in the high humidity of the day, before looking over at me. "Mom said you spent the night at the twins'?"

I grunt. "Word travels fast."

She flashes a smile. "I'm the favorite daughter now."

"Ha! Not until Rob puts a ring on that bare finger of yours."

I grimace as soon as those biting words leave my mouth.

"Yeah, well. Suppose keeping a man is half the battle for you."

I cover my mouth, but a snort still escapes me before I devolve into chuckling. "Ouch. Damn, girl."

Brandy chortles, too, our laughter fading into the drone of cicadas. "What happened, anyway?"

"Nothing happened. I couldn't sleep, went out for a drive, gave Z's drunk ass a ride when I saw him walking home from the bar, and passed out at their place. Nothin' to it."

Brandy barks out a laugh, stopping at her car. "I don't

believe that one bit." She lowers her head slightly and asks, "Did you and Zak hook up?"

I let out a long, loud groan, walking away. "No, we did not."

A lifted pickup passes by, honking at us. Probably warning us to move along since we parked in a no-parking zone.

I stop at my car, turning to find Brandy still eyeballing me suspiciously.

I make a face, almost whining and stamping my foot at her. "Nothing happened!"

She looks me up and down, making a sassy face back at me. "Just surprised to hear Zak didn't say or do anything."

Given what I did to him, asking why would be a dumb question as Brandy hops into her car. But I was there last night—I think him trying to refuse to let me take him home was about all he could muster through the shock and drunkenness.

As long as I don't have to admit that I actually hooked up with Adrian last night.

The handle of my car is already hot to the touch, but my hand lingers when trees rustle in my periphery. When I turn to look over my shoulder, the owl suddenly bursts through, soaring into the air.

I rub my eyes and blink a few times.

I swear, I saw dark hair on its head.

Chapter 10

Dead to Me

–DED

Every time I blink, the deer's flayed guts flash behind my eyelids. I searched for Gigi's profile online to message her about it, telling her what Brandy and I found, and she messaged back saying she was already on the way with her boyfriend to check things out.

The message she sends while I'm stopped at a light on the way to Shannon's makes me double take.

Something dragged it off.

A picture of the approach shows no deer. Just a gigantic bloodstain painting the approach and the chalk pentacle a dark crimson. Even the whiskey's gone.

I think ik what's going on. Someone is playing the devil to stir up panic. Bet.

A horn honks behind me, and I toss my phone aside.

It's hard to push aside thoughts of ritual sacrifice and the deer and whiskey no longer being at the bridge when I arrive at Shannon's and Kris's new place not too far from the

Ramos botanica. Before I left, everyone was still at the Ramos estate, but I guess Kris and Shannon finally had enough of sharing a house with two bachelors and she let the twins have the house since they're forever joined at the hip and have to share everything, anyway.

Including you, apparently.

I growl at myself for the thought, bitching nonsensically until I climb out of my car in front of a faded yellow folk Victorian house with a red brick patio and teal metal columns.

The screen door suddenly swings open.

A little girl who is a lot bigger than I remember sprints out the front door toward me—the flash of bright red and long dark hair is unmistakable.

As soon as I step onto the curb, she screams for me. "Abby!"

There's barely enough time to squat before Andrea flings herself at me. Just like her tio, she's solid and knocks the wind out of me, almost pushing me clean over onto my butt.

"When did you get so big?" I exclaim, arms hugging her small frame tightly. "Oh, my goodness, sweetheart."

"You've been gone *forever*, Abby!"

I'm not sure why this is the thing that rips my heart out of my chest and tears it into tiny pieces that I couldn't possibly pick up and glue back together.

A sob escapes my chest, and tears leak down my nose as I bury my face in her curly brown hair, holding her more tightly.

"Abby? Are you okay?"

Choking back sobs, I lift her from the ground and pivot away from the house when Shannon and Kris emerge, desperately hugging onto this little girl I've called niece since before she was even born. She might've been a surprise born to teen parents, but she's always been the highlight of our lives. Just when we thought we couldn't push through for another show, Kris would text us all a photo or video of Drea encouraging us to keep going, and it would give us all the strength to do what we do best, even if it hurt.

When I finally sniffle, I kiss her head, stroke her long hair, and murmur, "Yeah, I'm okay."

Rocks clack a few feet away. When I open my eyes, I find Zak staring at me with the greatest ache pulling his features into a sour, heartbroken frown. I'm not sure if it's from me being here or from remembering all the hopes and dreams we talked about of having a little girl of our own.

I have to push those thoughts aside as I set Drea down on the ground, stooping to her level. I quickly swipe at the tears still streaking down my face.

Andrea stares at me worriedly with big brown eyes. With her sporting a bright red tulle skirt and sparkly matching crown, the tears dry.

I can't cry in front of a princess. Or her tio, who I know is still watching.

"So where's your puzzle at, huh? Think I owe you some help with one." I make a thoughtful face. "Or a million."

Andrea beams, grabbing my hand and whisking me away quickly enough so I don't see Zak's face.

"Hey, Kris!" I greet, laughing as her mini-me drags me toward the backyard.

Her only response is a forced, tight-lipped smile.

Andrea doesn't give me any time to wonder, already telling me exactly where to sit on the patio overlooking an above-ground pool on brown, dead grass. A two-hundred-and-fifty-piece puzzle is spread out on a glass tabletop.

That little girl would force me to sit right next to her constantly-shirtless tio Adrian, whose cheeks lift until they're touching his dark aviators.

And that damn tio would place his hand on my thigh, kiss my temple, and murmur, "Hey, baby."

I make a stink face at his glowing complexion before Andrea claps her hands, demanding my attention.

"Abby! You're here for me, not Tio Dree."

"Yes, ma'am." I jab my thumb in Adrian's direction, leaning closer to her to say, "I think you gotta make it clear to him, too."

The terrific death glare she gives must have been learned from her mother and subsequently perfected. "Tio, leave Abby alone."

Adrian's hand finally leaves my thigh when he throws his hands up. "Okay, mija."

The smirk loaded on his lips hides a devilish satisfaction when the backdoor swings open and Kris, Shannon, and Zak join us.

Shannon barbecues with a beer in hand, showing off his farmer tan with a weirdly pale-ass torso for someone married into a river rat family. The twins and Kris discuss whatever event is going on at their family botanica later this evening, something about a workshop by a visiting curandero.

I'm distracted by whoever is staring at me and making my skin crawl—probably the Ramos twin speaking as little as humanly possible and already nearing the end of his first beer, tapping his tattooed and ringed fingers against the bottle—as Andrea babbles about the last puzzle she did, the next puzzle she has picked out, and school.

She looks up at me with literal sparkles in her eyes. "Can we have a puzzle night? With snacks from the fruteria like we used to with Mama and DeeDee?"

It's hard fighting off angry tears when I notice the table falls silent. Angry that I've let her grow up so much without me. That being in the middle of the Ramos-Dempster family now makes me feel like a total stranger instead of part of it like I've always been.

I reach out to pinch her cheek, wrinkling my nose at her as if I'm making a face, but it's really to help blink away the burning in my sinuses. "Of course we can."

I won't tell her Brandy hates my guts now, and her mama probably does, too.

"You still like raspas and churros, or are you getting into Hot Cheetos and queso yet? Or piccadilly like Abby and Mama?"

"If you woulda picked up the phone and called once in a while, you'd know," Kris jabs in a firm voice.

I bite down on my bottom lip as I stare at Drea. I grab her hand and squeeze it gently before leaning closer. "You know Abby's very sorry, right?"

"Pinche—"

"Callate!" Adrian pipes up quickly. He gestures toward Andrea. "No enfrente de la princesita."

"Kris, come make y'all's plates," Shannon says sharply, cutting off the next thing she has loaded that stifles the air even more than the humidity and the clouds still rolling in.

I hang back, letting Kris leave the table first with Andrea, hoping it'll give her a moment to chill out. But Adrian grabs my hand and drags me inside the house.

He pushes me forward, toward his sister radiating hatred in my direction. "C'mon," he coaxes, handing me a paper plate. "Don't be shy."

I press myself a little too closely into Adrian's blazing side to avoid even risking bumping into Kris.

Something pinches my ass and I jolt away.

I take a small step back toward cabinets and glare daggers at Adrian, especially when he snickers quietly with a sly grin.

He points at the food on the kitchen counter. "Shannon's gotten a lot better at grilling."

"Yeah," Shannon calls out from the porch where he lingers with Zak, "so eat up, homegirl."

I chuckle, but the smirk immediately falls off my face when I note Zak's glower. I'm not sure which is worse: Kris's underhanded jabs, or Zak glaring at me nonstop.

"Now I've got the part that won't start fighting," I begin after chowing down and helping Andrea with a quarter of the puzzle before Shannon insisted she go swimming with her mama. "What the fuck is going on with the band?"

Chapter 11

Texas Cries

–Element Eighty

Adrian is a little too comfortable with his arm over my chair. "You know. Creative differences."

"Bullshit," I sneer, glaring at him. "We all know that's a stupid excuse for whatever is really going on."

"Sparrow didn't offer another contract," Shannon admits, leaning forward to rest his elbows on the table. "Think they caught wind of the actual creative differences and are letting things end naturally."

"Let what end naturally, exactly?" I question with brows raised sky high, daring him to say it.

He doesn't hesitate. "The band, Steph."

I stare until Shannon averts his gaze.

"So what are the actual creative differences, huh? Someone's got one foot out the door?" I glare specifically at Adrian and Zak. "Or are y'all having a lovers' quarrel with your BFF that can't be contained to sessions and meetings?"

The guys fall silent and, finally, all eyes are off me. I breathe a sigh of relief before laying into them further. "What happened in Atlanta?"

Shannon shifts in his seat. "I told you: Rob picked a fight with the twins and got 'em all arrested."

"Why?" I clarify. "Why'd he pick a fight?"

"He blamed us for you quitting and avoiding everyone," Zak says in a tone laden with contempt. "His little sister refused to come to the show, and he took it out on us."

Now, it's my turn to fall silent.

Zak's right—I told Shannon and Robbie both I wasn't going to be there. No matter how much either of them begged, I didn't want to be near the twins. I didn't want to be around anyone from my past life because the temptation to come back was too great.

Just fucking look at me now.

"So why are you suddenly here and getting up into band business?"

My head snaps up and I gawk at Zak. "Excuse me?"

"You bailed on us," he starts. Tattooed hand over tattooed fist, he leans toward me, glowering under yellow-tinted sunglasses. His tattooed muscles flex and bulge in a sleeveless Pantera shirt. "You quit the band and left town without warning or an explanation. What makes you think you can show up now and start runnin' your mouth?"

I sit back, almost stunned.

Almost.

"Pardon me for taking an interest in figuring out what the fuck has gone so wrong before it all royally implodes."

Zak's jaw tics. He points a finger at me. "You left," he pronounces. The muscles in his jaw twitch as his nostrils flare. "That's what went so wrong with Timeless." He hammers his finger into the tabletop with each word. "You. Fucking. Left."

My own jaw clenches, grinding my teeth to a fine powder as I cross my arms. "You sayin' that as my former bandmate or as my ex-boyfriend?"

Drea bursts through the door in a red bathing suit, giggling up a storm that breaks some of the tension at the table. Kris follows behind with her dark hair piled up in a high bun. She wears a lime green bikini that shows off her curvy petite figure and tattoos on her ribs and thigh.

I turn to find Shannon staring and smack his arm. "Chill with that or you'll have another kid runnin' around here, huh?"

Shannon simpers, still ogling his wife. "I was just thinkin' Drea should probably have a sibling by now."

"Not happening!" Kris yells.

"Aw, c'mon, mama," Shannon hollers back with his arms spread wide and a grin brightening his face. "We ain't gettin' any younger!"

Chuckling and glancing up, Zak still stares at me with a scowl. Metal scrapes loudly against concrete when he suddenly pushes away from the table and disappears inside the house.

"Dad!" Andrea calls for Shannon, who immediately abandons the table.

Leaving me alone with Adrian.

My fingertips drum incessantly against the glass in an erratic pattern while he taps away on his phone.

"Where's your *girlfriend*?" I hiss.

Adrian faces me. Even though I can't see his eyes behind his sunglasses, I can feel them trying to explore what I keep pushing him away from.

The corners of his lips turn upward. "Right beside me."

My eyes widen. "*Excuse me?*"

He snorts before turning his attention to his phone. "You heard me."

"What happened to Norma, huh?" I seethe through gritted teeth.

"I broke up with her." He pauses. "Sorry about that, by the way."

I lean back in my chair, resting my chin on my hooked thumb and covering my mouth threatening to foam. "What, so you think that's how it works?"

Adrian groans softly, resituating in his chair and leaning a little bit more closely toward me, but he keeps his focus on the house ahead of us. "Look, Steph. If you're back, I want a fair chance."

Scoffing, my hand falls and I glare at him. "Oh, really? You didn't even fucking ask me, asshole. Never mind even mention that you're seeing someone."

The backdoor swings open, and Zak steps through with a cold beer in hand. His searing gaze lands on me.

Adrian gives me his full attention and says quietly, "Fine. Will you be my girlfriend?"

I roll my eyes and grunt in response before pushing away from the table, heading to hang out with the girls. I'm not going to acknowledge whatever pathetic attempt that was.

Drea greets me with a splash that catches part of my tank top, and her dad chastises her.

"I don't know, Shan," Kris interrupts, glaring at me. "I think it's fair."

Shannon shakes his head in disapproval. "Don't start."

"Kris, I'm sorry—"

"For what, exactly? Abandoning your friends and family, or breaking my brother's heart? Or are you trying to keep the peace and make false promises long enough so you can disappear again next week?"

"Alright," Shannon grunts, gesturing for Andrea to go to him. "How about a water gun fight with your tios, huh?"

"Don't you even care about what you did?"

My brows furrow. "I... I..." Stammering, words flee from

my brain when I need them most. "I thought I was doing what was best."

"And what was that?" Kris says sharply, crossing her arms.

Shannon grabs Andrea and pulls her as far away from the pool as he can.

"You thought running away would solve everything, and you'd be able to show up out of the blue like nothing happened?"

I cross my arms and lean my weight onto one heel. "What, just like you did when you abandoned your new husband and daughter when you had your episode?"

Kris's dark eyes narrow on me, and her nostrils flare. But she doesn't say anything.

"We'll call it even, then," I say.

"No," she replies firmly. She gestures toward Shannon and Andrea. "Say sorry to my daughter who cried for *months* missing her weekly aunty date. Say sorry to Brandy for being a shitty friend and leaving her in the dust. Say sorry to Zak for breaking his heart because—" she throws her arm in the direction of the backdoor, glaring that way, "—he's never gotten over it."

"Kris, don't be startin' shit—"

"This has nothing to do with you," she yells back at her husband, giving him a death glare before turning it back to me. "Don't think you can waltz back into our lives like nothing happened."

My fingernails dig into my palms, reminding me to calm the fuck down and not let things boil over in front of Andrea. "I'm sorry," I reiterate before storming off toward the backdoor.

"You don't get to walk away," Kris shouts. Water splashes.

Shannon yells for his wife as I near the house.

But she's quick.

The roots of my hair burn when Kris grabs a fistful of it and throws me to the ground. She starts swinging.

All three guys swear, "Oh, shit!" over Kris's frustrated growls and cussing.

I try pushing her off, but, fuck, if she doesn't have her claws deep in my hair. Kicking and rocking doesn't help—she's well-versed in brawls from high school. She might be tiny, but it's made her learn how to handle herself around those taller and bigger.

Kris busts one cheek and scratches the shit out of the other with her extra-long acrylics before she suddenly flies off.

My face stings, and I lie on the crunchy grass with stinging clouds covering my eyes.

A figure towers over me.

"Kris, back off!" Zak barks.

He yells something that I can't make out over my nerves firing off and blaring in my ears like a squealing amp.

My bottom lip trembles as I sniffle, willing myself not to start sobbing in front of everyone.

Zak leans over me, and I blink.

He holds out his hand.

Blurriness consumes my vision as I push myself up from the ground and run inside. Lava finally bursts from my eyes, salty tears stinging the scrape on my cheek.

The door slams behind me, but it reopens and closes not even a couple of seconds after.

I brace myself. "Kris, I can't—"

"It's me, babe."

CHAPTER 12

ALMOST EASY

–AVENGED SEVENFOLD

HEARING ZAK'S VOICE—HIM CALLING ME "BABE" after all this time, sober—sends a razor-sharp blade through my heart, making lava turn into a waterfall. I can't sniffle fast enough.

"Why do you keep calling me that?" I question in a high-pitched whine as tears fall. I throw my hands in front of my face to hide.

Before I can even think about running, a blistering hot arm wraps around my shoulders, like the sun itself is giving me a hug.

"Old habit, I guess."

Zak leads me into the kitchen. His hands come to my hips, planting me solidly against a counter. "Stay put." He resituates his sunglasses on top of his head and opens a cabinet. "Let me patch you up. Kris got you pretty good."

I scoff, crossing my arms and staring at the tile floor with a trembling lip as tears tumble.

Zak's tattooed and ring-adorned hand appears, gently lifting my chin to make me look at him. Having those golden-brown eyes watch me with a grimace is so much more painful than Kris trying to beat the shit out of me. I'd rather let her finish the job than let Zak tenderly dab at my face and steal glances.

"Wish you'd stop cryin', Steph," Zak murmurs. The pads of his fingers brush tears away. "Kris doesn't punch *that* hard."

Damn guy still knows how to make me chuckle.

The corner of his mouth pulls up in a small, lopsided smile as he gingerly places a bandage over the cut.

God, he's still so fucking cute.

He lingers on my cheek for a moment too long before clearing his throat and letting his hands fall. "She shouldn't have done that."

"Yeah, well. Guess we've had a fistfight brewing between us for a while now." My head shakes again. "I should go."

"You comin' to the gig tonight?"

I pause. "Figured after last night's fiasco y'all wouldn't play."

"It's not so bad some nights." He searches my face. "I'd really like for you to be there. If you don't have anything better to do, I mean."

Fucking Christ.

I have to gnaw on my bottom lip before it has the chance to jut out again. A snivel slips, though, and my face crumples.

Zak's brows knit together, and he reaches up to swipe falling tears away again. "C'mon, don't do that. You really gonna let my tiny-ass sister make you cry in front of Drea?"

I step away to where he can't reach me with those goddamn tender hands of his. "It's not because of her."

We both fall silent, the air thick with humidity over Shannon and Kris bickering, Adrian and Andrea starting a water gun fight. Thunder rolls, and I sniffle.

"Just come tonight, babe. Me 'n' Adrian will behave, promise."

I make a face at him. "Why do you want me there? You, of all people." I scoff. "All of this is my fault, anyway."

The quick moment of hesitation doesn't escape me. "I've always wondered what it'd be like to see you in the crowd instead of on stage with me."

The frown returns, but I nod. "Okay." Staring up at Zak, getting lost in those eyes I used to could stare at for hours on end, I blurt, "You weren't drunk last night because of me, were you?"

Zak groans, rubbing his forehead. "Dree told me you picked me up and brought me home, but I don't remember any of it."

"Sure smelled like you wouldn't, anyway," I respond as I pivot for the front door.

Zak says from right behind me, "Thanks for takin' me home, babe."

"Sure thing, hon."

I wince when it feels like my heart plummets further into the abyss, wondering what the fuck is wrong with us both.

Zak follows me outside to my car. He watches carefully, like I'm a wisp of smoke that will disappear in the slightest breeze at any second.

Part of me wants to reach out, to grab his tattooed hand, tell him I'm right here, and I'm not going anywhere. Another part of me wants to drop down onto the crispy grass that will pierce the skin of my knees like needles to beg for his forgiveness, to tell him how sorry I am, how much I've regretted everything I've done. And the rest of me wants to get into my car, start driving, and never turn back because I know goddamn well no amount of apologizing and groveling will undo all the damage I've done, so I might as well quit while I'm ahead before I get my hopes up way too high.

Zak's eyes harden and his jaw clenches, quelling the boil back down to a simmer and making me swallow the words before I can retch it all up.

"Why didn't you post Rob's bail?" he questions.

I shrug. "Thought he could use a timeout." Before he has a chance to ask anything else about Atlanta, I quickly ask, "Do you know what's going on at the bridge?

Zak shakes his head and crosses his arms. "No."

"I ran into Gigi last night and she said shit's pickin' up again around the bridge with offerings and whatever. And Brandy and I found the black deer we saw last night gutted on the approach earlier. Like, sacrificed in a ritual."

The deer's bloody guts, the owl and its beak turned crimson stain my memory.

"I swear, I don't know anything about that. I—I remember bailing with Shannon. I had him drop me off at the bar on the way." His expression turns sheepish. Probably because the bar isn't on the way back to his place or Shannon's. "And, yeah, I drank enough to make me forget that I saw you last night." His eyes bore into mine, probing deeply. "I wasn't sure if you'd ever come back. I thought for sure you'd get Robbie from jail, but you never showed up."

My face falls. "You… you wanted to see me?"

"You're the girl I proposed to on stage at New Year's Ball after the best show I've ever played in my life," he starts with a straight face, matter-of-factly. "The same girl that embarrassed me in front of everyone over something I knew—*I knew*—was a sure thing. Who fuckin' cheated on me with my brother and wouldn't own up to her mistake. Just—" he throws his hands up, "—ducked outta town without any warning and blocked me on socials and wouldn't text or call either of us back."

Grimacing, my eyes close. I let the heat from my hands burn my arms in a desperate attempt to hold it all together.

"I wanted you to see how well we were doing without you. How well *I* was doing without you."

Tears slip on the sharpness of Zak's words that puncture right in my chest. With each pump, my heart hemorrhages straight into my lungs.

"I'm glad you never came because then you would've seen how much of a fucking lie that was."

I gasp sharply, eyes cracking opening to find him stalking away toward the house and slamming the door shut.

CHAPTER 13

TRUTH

–SEETHER

MAYBE ZAK HAD THE RIGHT IDEA LAST NIGHT getting drunk off his ass to forget seeing me.

Unfortunately for me, the bartender across the street from where their gig is in a couple of hours has a weak pour and, with the hundred degree temperature seeping into the bar and melting the ice in my margarita, all I'm doing is hydrating instead of drowning my guilt.

I just want something to push me all the way into oblivion, to drop me off about two months ago when everything glittered gold with a dream roster of clients on Dirty Peach's schedule, before Timeless came to Atlanta.

Sighing heavily, I let my head roll back and relish the gentle breeze from an AC vent above blowing over my face. I feel like I haven't slept in a couple of months because I haven't.

The first three albums played in my head over and over until I was reliving studio time with every blink. Stage lights and headbanging crowds flashed behind closed eyelids until I gave up trying to sleep and watched old Timeless shows and music videos, helplessly chasing the high of the stage through a screen.

I would pick up a guitar in the studio when no one was looking. I could never play, though—I wasn't in Timeless, and my fingers refused to cooperate and play anything at all.

I did my best to ignore their Atlanta show, but Shannon and Robbie both wouldn't let me forget about it, texting, calling and asking if I'd be there. Hell, even Ty talked about going, but I think that was mostly so he could show off the fact I was with him and not them.

Going to that show only would've gotten my hopes up, and I didn't want to have them dashed by a vindictive ex.

Not that I didn't deserve it.

But no matter how many hours I put in at the studio, all I could think about was Timeless, New Year's Ball, home. I convinced myself I could smell barbacoa and mesquite and cedar, crispy burnt grass and dusty dry clay until my stomach ached so badly that I cried myself right into San Antonio.

I love Atlanta. Hell, to some extent, I know Ty is right—I belong there more than San Antonio. The nonstop texts from my Dirty Peach musicians asking when I'll be back to record and hang confirms it.

But, goddamn it, San Antonio is my home.

Timeless is my band.

But I'm *not* Adrian's girlfriend.

Cold beads of condensation drip over my fingers, the margarita in my hand completely melted. My phone lights up with a notification.

I grab it and tap away until I'm on his social profile, looking at his blank relationship status.

It takes sifting through his friends list and mutuals until I find Norma.

Ladies, here's your fair warning the Timeless twins are off the market for the foreseeable future, her first public post reads. *A certain blonde guitarist is back in town.*

I snort, chuckling inappropriately before knocking back the rest of this watered down margarita that's making me sadder. If Adrian immediately confessed to Norma that he cheated on her, it's safe to say he confessed our misdeed to his brother after I bailed.

The smirk falls off my face, realizing that I'm the reason why this poor girl is having a really shitty day. *God, you really are a piece of shit.*

Haven't I seen pictures of her online? Or seen posts of them together? She looks vaguely familiar.

I keep scrolling until I find it: she tagged Adrian in a relationship status update just a couple of months ago. The like button is highlighted, displaying that me and a couple hundred others liked it. There's a picture of her kissing his cheek I try tapping on, but an error pops up: *Post not found.*

"Can I get you another?"

My attention snaps up to the bartender.

His brows knit together. "You okay?"

Warmth rolls down from the corner of my eye and traces the outline of my cheek. I quickly dash it away and reach for my purse. "I'm good."

Maybe Adrian and I deserve each other.

A line already wraps around the corner with people sporting Timeless merch at a venue that hosts big names in an intimate bar setting. I even spot a couple of Timeless-themed tattoos hiding in the shadows, away from the rain sprinkling from the sky.

I rap on the backdoor of the venue with our old "let me in" secret knock.

The heavy metal thing flings open. "Even when you're not in the band, you're still one of the first ones here," Shannon says.

The door slams behind me with a metallic *clank* as I follow him into a dim, cool hallway crammed with black cases and trunks with TIMELESS spray-painted in white across all of them.

"At least one of y'all are responsible without me around, huh?"

Shannon grabs a random roll of duct tape and a neatly-wrapped cord from a trunk and keeps heading toward the stage. "You leavin' was a kick in the ass for all of us."

My heart sinks. "I'm sorry."

He spins around suddenly, flashing me a pretty smile all the fans swoon over. "Didn't say it was a bad thing."

My stomach plummets. *Kick me while I'm down, why don't you...*

"Besides." He begins to unroll the cord and hooks up a board. "It finally got Zak to write something." Shannon chuckles to himself. "Figures it'd be the one song fans want us to play every show."

My brows furrow. "*Zak* wrote something?"

"Yeah, that's what I said when he showed up with it." He pauses, peering at me curiously. "Didn't you get those packages I sent you?"

I nod. "Yeah."

His brow, scarred from a piercing long closed, quirks. "I'm guessing you never opened them."

Chewing on the inside of my lip, I hate to admit, "I peeked inside, and when I saw it was Timeless stuff, I just... I packed it away."

I groan softly, rolling my eyes at myself. Shannon was just being a good friend, and here I am being extra shitty even to him.

"I'm sorry. It wasn't you. I just didn't want anything to do with the band."

His face goes blank for a split second before light

reignites in his eyes. "I get it." His focus returns to the board, fiddling with some switches. "Guess now you're here you might open 'em, huh? If you still got 'em, anyway."

"Yeah, of course I still have 'em. Mighta been band shit, but *you* still sent it."

"Glad to know I'm not on your shit list, ha."

I throw my arms around his slim waist since his shoulders just about clear my head and hug him closely. "You will never be on that list. Just hope I'm not on yours, either."

He squeezes me hard. "Never." Shannon steps away and has an odd look on his face. He holds up a hand and pinches his fingers together. "Just one little thing, Steph."

Oh boy. I know that papa bear look all too well.

"Don't go makin' false promises to Drea," he says in a tight voice. His features are hardened by an underlying resentment I haven't seen since Kris disappeared. "Kris wasn't lyin' that she cried for months after you left. You remember her cryin' for her mama when we couldn't get her to understand why she hadn't come back in so long."

My nose scrunches from holding back tears. I sniffle, crossing my arms and resituating my weight.

"'Abby' isn't just because she couldn't say aunty," Shannon continues. "Abby means aunty and godmother, and in her own special way, it means mama, too. You stepped up when Kris couldn't be the mother Drea needed. So you walkin' out the way you did destroyed us both."

My head hangs. Staring at the faded blue rug covering cords running across the stage can't erase the sulk from my face.

"You're still my best friend, Steph. But don't go promising shit to our girl if you're not gonna stick around."

He twists around for another cord, resuming preparations for sound check.

I take a step closer. "And..." I trail off.

The question is at the tip of my tongue, something I've wanted to hint at since I made the decision to come back.

I can't swallow it down this time.

I search Shannon's hazel eyes. "And if I am?"

He reaches for his back pocket and hands me a lanyard with laminated cardstock shouting VIP in big, bold letters underneath the Timeless tour graphic. The muscles in his jaw twitch. "Prove it."

Slipping it over my head, I ask, "Need help with anything?"

"You gonna touch Zak's guitar?"

I hesitate. It's a simple task, tuning and playing a guitar for the back-of-house engineer to adjust settings, but touching Zak's equipment? "Doesn't he have a tech?"

"He's just like you, ya know. If he didn't touch it, then it ain't perfect."

I hide a small smile behind my hand. That's something I've always loved about him: he's hands-on and keeps at it until it's perfect.

Both on stage and in bed.

My cheeks flush.

"Damn, Steph," Shannon comments. "The hell you thinkin' about that's makin' your face so red?"

My eyes widen. "Nothing."

He grins, chortling. "I see you, girl." The look drops from his face suddenly as he focuses on situating a pedal board just right. "Heard about Dree and Norma."

I clear my throat quietly, swallowing the rock that suddenly appeared. "I, uh... I didn't know he was seeing someone."

"Ah."

I cross my arms and pivot slightly, watching people moving in the shadows beneath the bright stage lights. Cords are tossed. Boards hooked up. Loose bits taped down or hidden underneath rugs. Toms rigged to kick drums and pedals situated.

My arms slap against my legs. "Look, I don't know what to say here—"

"Nothing," Shannon interrupts. "I already know too much."

"What do you know?"

"They're my wife's brothers, you know." He kneels at my feet to tape down the corner I stepped on. When he looks up at me, he squints against the brightness of the lights overhead. "I know y'all so damn well that I know which one a y'all fuckin' fart in the van even if it doesn't make a sound. I think I knew before you did, Steph." He scoffs, muttering, "I think we all did."

"She can be pretty clueless sometimes," a familiar voice says.

Robbie suddenly appears in the bright lights, hopping up on stage. He slings an arm around my shoulders, yanks me close, and musses my hair. "She don't know dick from shit."

I grunt and shove him away. Good thing my hair isn't done, just tossed up in a bun.

When I catch a glimpse of his face, my jaw drops a little.

"Didn't know you'd be here," he says as he pinches my side.

I shrug, not bothering to mention the reason why I'm here. "You look like shit, bro."

He studies the bandage on my cheek and points at it. "Twinsies." He then gestures toward the back. "Make yourself useful and watch the door. Ain't cool walkin' in through the front."

Making a face at him, I glance at Shannon and he puts a finger to his lips to silently shush me, nodding and cocking his head, telling me to go.

"Assholes," I grumble as I head to the back.

Perching on a sturdy trunk by the backdoor, I whip out my phone. I hesitate over the screen, but it flows so naturally when I start to type in the search bar.

Zak Ramos, Timeless.

Promo and concert images of Zak and his shimmering white guitar display first. I tap one to look at it more closely, one of Zak shouting at the crowd and riling them up. The photo links to an interview of Zak talking about the song he wrote.

Scanning the article, confusion knits my brows together and pulls the corners of my lips downward. Zak never wrote lyrics when I was in the band since he sucked at poetry and hated toying with words, so he left that up to me and Shannon.

My heart sinks.

Metal Music News: "Dawn" is your debut writing a song completely by yourself and it's a fan favorite. It's heart-wrenching and seems to come from a place of deep pain. Do you think you'll write more for Timeless after this? Or has the positive fan response made you shy away from writing anything else?

Zak Ramos: Yeah, it's ironic I write this and now that's all anyone wants. Sorry to disappoint, but I'm hoping this is a one-time thing. I just had a lot of shit to work through and I'd like to think I'm over it after getting it out the way I know best: through music.

A familiar rapping sounds from the door, making me jump and drop my phone. I snatch it up before pushing the metal bar to open the door.

I groan. "Really?"

Adrian grins and sets his aviators on top of his head. "Hey, baby."

CHAPTER 14

WE WILL GO DOWN

–DREAM DROP

ADRIAN'S BEAM IS SO FUCKING ANNOYING AS HE steps inside, practically on me as the the door slams shut behind him. He leans down, but I turn my head and back away.

"Fuckin' nope."

But he grabs me, forcing me to stay still as he plants his mouth on mine.

I growl with fists balled up at my sides.

His smirk is more pronounced when he finally parts. "Nice seein' you here."

A conniving smile forms on my lips. "Yeah. Zak asked me to come."

His expression falls. "Don't you think I want you here, too?"

"You didn't ask."

"It was *heavily* implied."

I roll my eyes and push him away to sit on the trunk.

He forces himself between my legs, and his hands cup my face to make me look up at him. "Are you and Zak working things out?" he questions.

Bristling, I attempt to shake his hands away, but his hold is firm. "Not that I'm aware of."

Adrian studies me carefully, like he's memorizing every pore and imperfection on my face. His fingers gently trace the bandage on my cheek.

"Why?" I ask.

He tips my chin upward and leans down. He kisses me softly. Repeatedly.

Last night, his touch was bullish and frantic. This morning, it was decisive and assertive. Now, it's tender and adoring and sends a quiver through my stomach until my inner walls clench.

"You're mine this time around, princesa," he finally murmurs over my lips.

I shove him away. "I already told you no."

Adrian gazes longingly, searching for something in my eyes. "What will it take for you to say yes?"

My gaze drops to Adrian's hands, making out TIME on the right fingers and LESS on the left. When I blink, the nightmare that's been haunting me flashes in the brief darkness, reminding me that I didn't come home after seeing Zak's heart break almost every night on repeat for so long just to do it all over again.

I don't say a word. I push my back against the cool, hard brick and cock my head toward the stage where sound check is in progress with people yelling at each other over adjustments. "You have a show to get ready for."

Adrian grasps my jaw, forcing me to look at him. "I want you, Steph," he insists quietly. "We owe each other this."

My brows knit together. "We owe Zak an apology."

"I apologized. You're the one who ran away without saying anything."

Swallowing hard, I say softly, "I'm gonna apologize, and I'm not gonna fuck it up this time."

His eyes narrow, glowering, but he doesn't say a word. He inhales sharply before grabbing his sunglasses from the top of his head and placing them on mine. Then, he reaches over his shoulder and grabs his shirt from his back, pulls it over his head, and lets it fall onto my lap.

I can't help ogling his bare, tattooed torso, eyeballing the piercing in his left nipple. I make my eyes snap shut, trying to shake the memory of last night out of my head. It only worsens when the darkness sends all sorts of sensations flooding my nerves and panties. "Get outta here with that shit. Fuck."

He taps my chin up and presses his lips to mine, the briefest sensation of warmth brushing over my lips before it disappears.

I lurch forward to recapture it, but Adrian is already down the hall, sashaying away. The canned lights overhead cast playful shadows in the curvature of his back and the dips just above the waistband of his black shorts make me salivate.

Huffing, I cross my arms and lean back against the wall, kicking the other side of the hallway in annoyance. I toss Adrian's shirt on top of the guitar boat beside me and set his sunglasses on top in a desperate attempt to get the scent of him the fuck away.

I didn't come back to hook up with Adrian, I tell myself. I *didn't* come back to hook up with Adrian.

But I did last night. And he's willing to do whatever it takes to make me his.

I stare at the black brick in front of me, considering the image of Zak playing his guitar burned into my retinas, the lingering taste of Adrian on my lips, until it hits me: the din of a crowd.

The doors have opened, and I'm still waiting for one last knock that has yet to sound.

Getting up to peek out the door, there's nada—nothing

but a freak bout of rain lightly wetting the bone-dry pavement of the small parking lot.

It's chaos by the stage with Adrian on the phone, Shannon and Robbie furiously bitching between themselves and a couple of others until Shannon catches sight of me and swoops in.

"Hey, he hasn't come by yet, has he?"

"No. No one's outside, either."

"Fuckin' A," he groans, scrubbing a hand over his face. "You mind waiting back there just in case?"

Adrian hangs up and starts another phone call, completely oblivious to anything besides getting a hold of his brother.

At the back door, I peek outside again. Still no one and nothing except heavier rain.

Each minute that passes by without any word from Zak, without hearing the secret knock on the door, sets me even further on edge. I ball up my hands to make myself stop picking at the skin around my nails, but even then, I find myself kicking the wall and trunk.

"Hey!"

My sight snaps to Shannon at the end of the hall, and I rush to meet him. "Is he here?"

Shannon shakes his head. "No. Adrian hasn't been able to get a hold of him, and neither have the rest of us."

Groaning softly, I check the time on my phone. Seven o' clock sharp.

"Timeless! Timeless! Timeless!" The crowd chants, echoing down the hall like a taunt.

"Goddamn it."

"What the fuck are y'all gonna do?" I question breathlessly with wide eyes.

The crowd starts hooting and hollering.

"Hey, y'all," a familiar voice sounds over the speakers.

"Sorry for the unconventional opening, but we're in a bit of a bind at the moment."

Shannon and I hardly glance at each other before making a run for the stage, colliding into each other to peer over Robbie's shoulder.

Adrian notices, his sight honing in on me. The corner of his mouth pinches into a smirk. "Zak's out for the night, but someone's here that I think could help out." Adrian gestures toward me, directing the crowd's attention. "Stephani Wade's in the house."

My jaw drops.

His sight sweeps over the crowd, glittering eyes unbothered by the bright stage lights. "Y'all think we can convince her to play for old time's sake?"

The crowd loses their fucking shit, hooting and hollering and starting to shout my name. Shouting for me to get on stage, to pick up the guitar again and play for them.

Adrian turns away from the mic, heading our direction on the side stage. The closer he comes, the darker my vision tunnels on him like we're the only two in here and not like hundreds of eyes are on us.

"Don't fucking do this to me," I fume.

"We're short a guitarist who knows Timeless songs," he states matter-of-factly. "Not sorry I'm lookin' out when you'd do the same."

The air inside the bar is muggy, like the sweltering humidity has fought its way inside to choke me as I search the faces of my former bandmates, their techs and roadies, fans waiting for me to make a move.

"Ste-pha-ni! Ste-pha-ni! Ste-pha-ni!"

My heart pummels against my sternum a million beats per minute. My hands are sweaty. Mouth is dry. Breath shaking. I think I see stars twirling in the periphery.

Staring at Adrian, I silently beg him not to encourage me

to go out on that stage, to not let me make another huge mistake thinking I can make things work.

Nightmares be damned, I shouldn't be here. Not without Zak.

Adrian steps closer. "This is why you're back, *princesa. This* is why you came back."

I look between Robbie and Shannon, both of them waiting with bated breath.

"Steph."

The smirk is gone from Adrian's face. All that's left are his pleading dark eyes. "You belong out there with us," he says, hardly audible above the crowd chanting my name.

"I don't even know any of the new songs," I reason.

"We can play an old school set," Shannon offers.

"You should be out there with us, Steph." My brother winces when his cheeks reach too high into two black eyes. "C'mon. It's not like you'll be stuck playing with us forever. It's just one night."

I swallow the hard rock in my throat. *It's just one night. For old time's sake.*

I gulp down a deep breath and reach for the VIP lanyard, slipping it off my neck and shoving the laminate into my back pocket.

"Where's his spare?"

CHAPTER 15

WHAT IF I LOST IT

—BLOODSIMPLE

MY EYES ARE WIDE ON THE CROWD ANTICIPATING Timeless on the stage any minute now. Zak's shimmering white guitar hangs from my shoulders while I'm huddled up on the side stage with Shannon, Robbie, and Adrian.

Fuck, fuck, fuck...

An arm wraps around my shoulders, setting them ablaze from the warmth of body heat. My stare breaks from the guitar to find Adrian watching me with a questioning look.

"You're not gonna run off in the middle of the set, are you?"

I gasp sharply, audible enough for Adrian to furrow his brows. "I don't think I can move."

Amusement fractures the seriousness of his features. He leans toward me, lips at my ear. "You got this. Pretend we're on tour from before you left and Zak got sick."

"Zak doesn't get sick!" I squeak.

Adrian chuckles and tugs at a lock of my hair that escaped the bun on my head. "He did just this once."

"A'ight," Shannon starts, clapping his hands and rubbing

them together. "Y'all remember the setlist from *Santa Muerte*?"

"Yeah," we all confirm.

"Cool. That should get us by tonight." Shannon focuses on me, brows raised high. "You ready, Steph?"

"No!" I exclaim.

"C'mon," he beckons, "you're the notorious Stephani Wade. You got this."

"Oh, God," I groan under a shaky breath as we all turn to face the darkened stage.

A hand grabs mine, squeezing hard. Adrian says in my ear, "You got this, princesa," before kissing my cheek and letting go to march out onto the stage with Shannon and Robbie, drumsticks in hand.

I leap forward to catch up, and the crowd hoots and hollers.

I'm here.

I'm on stage.

I'm on stage with my old band and my ex-boyfriend's unfamiliar guitar hanging from my neck and a breath stuck in my lungs that I can't quite let go of because *I keep doing things I thought I would never do again.*

Shannon releases an unholy growl from deep within his chest that shakes the venue.

Lights flash on, dancing across the stage and illuminating a jumping crowd. I don't have to look to know all eyes are on me.

And like riding a goddamn bike, my fingers dance across the fretboard, plucking a familiar riff I remember composing in our first practice space in high school.

A sea of phones and flashing lights take photos and video of my unexpected guest appearance, but I can't stop staring at my hands on Zak's guitar.

Eventually, my stare breaks, scanning the crowd before

looking over at my former bandmates for something. Anything. Some reassurance that I'm not royally fucking up songs we wrote together over ten years ago.

Robbie focuses on his bass between interactions with the crowd, mouthing words along with them. Shannon jumps up and down with the crowd, waving them on before hiking a leg up on an amp and bending over to scream from his diaphragm.

Adrian notices me desperately looking around as he beats his set, crashing cymbals between toms and the snare, powerhouses for legs pounding a double kick set. He smirks in a way that makes the breath caught in my lungs disappear completely before he points a drumstick in my direction and winks.

The first song ends with a literal bang.

The lights lower, and fans go wild.

Shannon saunters over and throws an arm over my shoulders, looking out over the crowd. "Steph's been gone a while, so she doesn't know any of our new shit by heart. So how about an old school set tonight? Y'all fuck with that?"

The hollers and screams the crowd responds with sends goosebumps flooding throughout my skin.

Every single one of my limbs is numb.

Flashes of blue and purple and green lights blur people and instruments together into one amalgamation.

Shannon's shrieks and growls scramble my brain until it pushes my face toward the microphone in front of me and I sing or scream with him, precisely on cue like I never forgot.

Adrian's percussive explosions set the pace for the beating in my chest.

A few fans that scream and headbang in front of me remind me where I am and what I'm doing when my mind starts floating out into the ether above the crowd.

I shouldn't be on this stage, but my head bangs as if I couldn't possibly be anywhere else.

"How'd she do tonight?"

Fans cheer, the sound consuming the entire venue and then some. Realizing they're cheering *for me*, I wave after I take a quick gasp of breath since I can finally breathe a little.

But the rhythm of my heart falters.

It's over already?

Shannon turns, facing me with a brilliant beam on his face. I haven't seen it from this angle in so long—a sight for sore eyes. "Thank you, Stephani," he says into the mic, almost tumbling over into his dad voice.

I laugh, giving the crowd a bow, and the lights cut off, allowing us to slip off stage.

"Holy shit," Shannon exclaims as soon as we step off stage. He throws an arm around my shoulders. "Steph, you still got it, girl!"

"Yeah, well," I start, glaring over at Adrian a little more playfully than I intended.

That shit-eating grin isn't coming off his face any time soon.

"It wasn't bad. I guess."

"You're a little rusty, but I bet one more show would get you back to the best of your heydays," Robbie says with his arms crossed over his chest. The gleam in his eyes is warm, saying what he doesn't say out loud: he missed me being on stage with him.

Even though I've burned everyone and thought I'd never play with Timeless again, it seems like they missed me. The guys, the fans—they all loved me being back.

I think they may even *want* me back.

Everyone except Zak, who practically stood me up tonight.

"Seriously, Steph," Shannon says. "Thanks for doing this. It was really great having you back out there."

Nodding, I make myself turn away before my guts spill out.

As I rush down the cool hallway, I already know he's following.

Bursting through the door, into the stormy night and the boiling rain, I start to run. I force myself to run faster, digging in my pocket for my keys to unlock my car, and not because of the rain drenching me from head to toe.

I slam the door shut just in time.

Adrian appears in the window and strikes against metal, making me jump. "Goddamn it, Steph. Open the door."

The backdoor of the bar swings open, distracting Adrian. I start the car and his wild eyes come back to me. Rain pours down his head, dripping onto his face and down his shirtless, toned torso.

"Where the fuck are you going?"

I crack the window so we don't have to yell and garner attention from passers-by. Rain trickles in. "I'm gonna go find Zak."

Adrian purses his lips, nostrils flaring. "Forget Zak."

I frown. "What if he's hurt somewhere?"

"He's fucking fine."

Staring at Adrian, I realize: "Why didn't he come with you tonight?"

"I don't fuckin' know. He was off doin' his own thing."

"You two always come together to gigs."

"Steph, you haven't been here in a while. You don't know shit anymore."

Glaring at him, I throw the car into drive. "Y'all are joined at the goddamn hip. Stop fucking lying."

He slaps the roof of my car and shouts as I spin off.

The rain falling in sheets over the windshield fragments

streetlights in weird, nebulous ways, especially when the realization sinks in: I just played guitar for the first time since that fateful NYB concert. I just played a Timeless show, and everyone fucking loved me.

Maybe… maybe I could make a comeback, after all. Maybe I could pick guitar back up and give music another shot—maybe I can rejoin Timeless.

Those thoughts come crashing down the longer I sit in traffic on the way back home as lightning streaks across the sky and rain beats down on the roof of my car.

The only reason why I went to the gig is because Zak asked me, and the only reason why I got up on stage tonight is because Zak didn't show. Adrian all but forced me out there with his brother's guitar in hand, acting none the wiser about his twin's whereabouts when they've arrived to a show separately *maybe* twice in ten years of playing gigs.

Turning on the road closer to home, a low, deep growl consumes the cab.

They fucking set me up.

They *planned* all this. They concocted this desperate scheme to make me get up on that stage, play, and ask to rejoin the band, to make it seem like it was all my idea.

And for what, just for Zak to fucking shoot the idea down at the end?

Anger fumes and boils over as I approach Losoya Bridge.

A familiar figure forms in the rain, stumbling on the side of the road.

The devil himself stops to face me as I swing the car door wide open after veering off the road to park.

"What the *fuck* are you doing out here?" I scream over the downpour as I stalk toward him on the other side of the road.

Zak blinks a few times, eyes glittering from lightning flashing across the sky, before focusing on me. He's soaked from head to toe.

His brows furrow, and confusion crosses his face. "Babe?"

I stare at him, mouth agape and catching droplets. "Would you fucking stop calling me that?"

"I'm... I'm sorry..."

Zak stumbles forward, and I catch his heavy ass before he takes a serious tumble.

Lightning flashes, and my eyes widen.

Blood flows down his neck and camouflages his tattoos. Following the crimson trail, two puncture wounds prick the flesh of his neck.

"Oh, my God!" I shriek, pulling him toward the car to lean him against it. My hands tremble as I try to examine the wound. Rain mixes with blood. "Z, what happened?"

He shakes his head. "Get outta here, babe."

I grab his shoulders. "I'm taking you to the hospital—"

Zak shoves my hands off and stumbles away. "No. You gotta get outta here. Right now."

I follow him, hands on his waist as he starts heading back toward the approach. "Zak, what the fuck is going on?"

He spins around suddenly and topples forward. I catch him, setting him straight, but he slaps my hands away. "You can't be here!" he yells with eyes that nearly glow in the darkness.

"Hon, you're hurt. You need to get checked out."

"So you can call me 'hon,' but I can't call you 'babe'?"

"Are you fucking kidding me? *That's* what you wanna argue about right now?" Eyeing the wound on his neck, I can't tell if the bleeding has stopped or if it's rain dripping down his neck. "Did you get bit by a fucking vampire?"

He looks over his shoulder. "Babe, leave."

"I'm not leaving you—"

A blood-curdling screech sounds from behind Zak in the dark. I drop to my knees, covering my head with my arms.

Wings flap right over me.

The owl screams above me and I yelp in response, swatting the thing away until arms encircle me. They drag me away and throw me into the car, slamming the door behind me.

Zak tosses himself into the passenger seat and slaps the dash. "Go!"

With the blur of pale white wings flapping through glimmering sheets of rain, he doesn't have to tell me twice to put the pedal to the metal.

Tires screech on the road as I turn around as fast as the car will let me.

Gasping for breath from my heart violently pummeling against my chest, I look in the rearview.

The streetlight at the bridge flips on for a brief second and lightning flashes, illuminating a dark silhouette where the owl was.

CHAPTER 16

HOLD ON

–ALL THAT REMAINS

MY EYES ARE WIDE ON THE DARK ROAD shimmering from the rain, completely alert and bewildered.

Neither of us say a word when I pull up to the Ramos house and shift the car into park. Eventually, Zak leans over to turn the ignition off before slumping back. Neither of us move or make a sound above the white noise of rain pelting the car.

"Zak, what the fuck was that?" I whisper.

I can't pry my stare from the entrance surrounded by spindly huisache trees. I'm not sure whatever—*whoever*—was on the bridge didn't follow us. We're right down the road, hardly half a mile away.

Something touches me, making me jump and snatch my arm away. I glare at Zak, but he's staring at my arm.

"Baby, you're bleeding," he says softly.

A nasty gash oozes shimmering crimson in the porch light, dripping down my flesh. I make a face when it starts to sting, and it worsens when goosebumps prickle my skin under Zak's scrutiny.

He's soaking wet, but I can still see the blood blanketing his neck and down chest.

"So are you." My face crumples and voice cracks. "Zak, what happened back there?"

"Babe, let's get inside and—"

"What happened?" I yell.

"Stephani, get your ass inside the goddamn house," he yells back. He glances at the entrance. "Now."

I don't know what he saw, but I'm not about to stick around to find out. So I grab my phone out of the cupholder and run into the storm.

Zak slams the heavy door shut behind us and swiftly locks it. I start to open my mouth, but Zak covers it with his hand. "We can talk *after* we're both fixed up, alright? Don't want either of us getting infections."

When I nod and he's assured I won't fly off the handle, he finally lets his hand drop.

Tears prick my eyes at the sight of his blood. I don't know if he was swaying because of blood loss or being drunk, but his flesh still has plenty of color.

"Promise you're okay." My voice wavers. "You're not gonna die on me."

"I promise."

I study the puncture wounds in his neck, blood smeared over his tattoos. "Hon, what the hell got you out there?"

He takes my hand and leads me to his side of the house. "We'll talk after, okay?"

The door suddenly bangs and something scratches on the other side, making us both jump and stumble backwards.

Screeching pierces through the stucco, grating my ears and sending ice down my spine.

Zak slips an arm around me and drags me to the left hallway. I look over my shoulder and down the hall, where whatever is outside screams and scratches at the front door.

I've heard enough stories to know what's out there.

"That… that's la lechuza! She…" I stare down at my arm when Zak turns lamps on with the flick of a switch in his room. "Oh, my God. She's real."

"Yeah, and real fuckin' pissed." He starts rifling through drawers. "I told you to leave."

My jaw drops. "I wasn't about to leave you out there!"

"Yeah, well," he starts, facing me and shoving a stack of clothes toward me. "Just this once, I wish you woulda."

I stare at the shirt and gym shorts in his hands. "What's this for?"

"You're not going back out there," Zak states. "Take a shower so I can get that gash patched up. And I gotta do a limpia."

Groaning, I stamp my foot. "I'm not staying here, and I'm not letting you rub an egg all over me—"

"Stephani," he bellows, "you're gonna do what I tell you, or I'll let la lechuza eat your goddamn heart in the driveway like you fuckin' deserve. Got it?"

I can still hear her, even from all the way back here in Zak's new goth bedroom, banging on the door, scratching and howling a hellacious cacophony. The ear-splitting sound pierces the air and sends tears welling up in my eyes.

Finally, I break the silence with a trembling voice. "Why do you care so much?"

Zak tosses the clothes at me before crossing his sinewy arms over his bloody chest. "Why the fuck do you?"

My nose scrunches and tears spill over hard and fast as I spin around and run down the hallway. La lechuza grows louder when I rush by; my nerves electrify and a shiver runs down from my skull.

I slam Adrian's bathroom door behind me and lock it. My forehead rests against the cool wood, and I snivel as tears drip to the tile floor.

I couldn't even make it a day back home without getting stuck with my ex-boyfriend and wearing his clothes. Without taking a shower and smelling like his brother who's trying his damndest to make me his girlfriend even though I fucking hate his guts.

The cut on my arm burns from soap. More tears fall as blood seeps and mixes with water running down the drain.

"Shut up. You're a big girl," I chide myself, willing the tears to stop so I can get the hell out. Being stuck with Zak for a night wasn't on my to-do list, but neither is making myself home on Adrian's side of the house after spending last night with him.

Besides, there are bigger problems out there than me being stuck with my ex for one night. Like la lechuza trying to get inside this house and rip me to shreds, and Zak walking around drunk and injured.

I catch myself in the mirror on the way out. The bleeding has slowed to a trickle on my arm. Thankfully, Zak's gained enough muscle that his shirt hides the Waffle House fifteen-plus I gained.

Break up just for him to get more tattoos, get all muscular...

The screeching has stopped, but there's still an incessant scratching at the door. The lights are off and rustling sounds from the kitchen.

"Z?" I call out.

His head pokes out from the kitchen, low light illuminating his dark, damp hair tied in a knot on top of his head. He gives a stern look as he holds a finger to his lips before gesturing for me to follow.

"Callate," Zak says in a hushed tone when I round the corner. "Maybe she'll give up if we don't make too much noise."

A first aid kit is laid out on the white quartz bar top with gauze, swabs, and medical tape, complete with a crystal glass holding brown liquid on the rocks.

I grab the glass, helping myself to a sip of what turns out to be amaretto. "Mm, thank God. Thought this was gonna be Crown."

Zak snorts as he reaches for my arm to inspect the cut. "Somethin' told me you were gonna steal my drink."

Instead of letting tears renew, I chew on my lip and nurse the amaretto as Zak applies antibacterial ointment. I always stole his drink and complained because I didn't like Crown, so he would switch it out for amaretto.

"You probably need stitches," Zak mutters, peering at the wound through glasses he wasn't wearing when I picked him up. "What're all these other scratches from?"

"When Brandy and I went to the approach."

He frowns. "You said y'all found a sacrificed deer, right?"

"Yeah. Gigi went to check it out earlier." I grab my phone from the pocket of his gym shorts I'm wearing and tap until I show Zak the picture she sent. "Obviously, somebody's acting the part as the devil and taking offerings."

He doesn't react to the photo, returning to dab ointment over my wound. "Might actually be the devil himself doin' it," Zak mutters.

I scoff, rolling my eyes. "Let me guess: you saw the devil on the bridge, too?"

He stays silent, pinching the gash on my arm together and lining up a series of butterfly bandages over it.

"You're the one behind the ritual shit," I say in disbelief.

Zak glances up at me and shakes his head. "No."

Scratching at the door turns into tapping.

I grimace, staring long and hard at the dark, oiled wood with black metal accents as I slowly set the crystal glass on the counter. "Doesn't the legend say la lechuza is a witch who made a deal with the devil?"

When Zak doesn't answer, I turn to find him watching the door, too. Eventually, he nods. "Yeah."

With him distracted, I make a run for the door.

"Stephani, *no*," he growls.

Peering out the small window, I catch only the briefest glance of the darkened entryway before Zak snatches me away.

It's her.

The owl I've been seeing is on the front porch, scratching at the door and crying like a baby. A huge, gigantic white owl, almost as big as me, but the face...

"Is that *Kris*?" I hiss as he pushes me toward the kitchen. "Your fucking sister is la lechuza?"

CHAPTER 17

ROPE

–40 BELOW SUMMER

A HEADACHE FORMS SOMEWHERE ABOVE MY TEETH and behind my eyes after seeing Kris Ramos-Dempster at the doorstep of the twins' place—la lechuza in the flesh.

"We thought she had it under control." Zak gingerly situates me by the bar. "Guess you visiting put her over the edge."

"What the fuck do you mean, 'we thought she had it under control'? When the fuck did this happen?"

"Remember when she went off the deep end and disappeared for a couple of months? Said she checked herself into psych?"

My expression turns severe, skin drawing taut. What I did to Zak may have set her off today, but what she did to Shannon is something I've never forgiven her for. She wasn't the one distracting Andrea with every single puzzle available between the store and secondhand shop. She wasn't the one making sure Shannon didn't turn back to old vices and had a shoulder to sob on when he didn't have to be strong for Andrea after she went to bed.

"Yeah," I reply through gritted teeth. "She said she was getting evaluated."

He presses gauze against my arm. "She was visiting our tias down in Mexico. I don't know what happened—she's never said how or why. I just know that's when the change happened and they knew how to help." He glances up at me. "Shannon's forgiven her. So should you."

"Shannon's a sweetheart obsessed with a hot-headed bitch," I spit, glaring at him.

Zak is gentle as he traces the gauze, sealing tape onto my skin, despite me speaking ill of his older sister.

"He deserved better than what she put him through. I don't care if she's his baby mama turned into a man-eating owl or whatever the fuck."

He grabs the amaretto from the counter and takes a step back as he sips. "So I deserved you cheating on me?"

"No." I cross my arms and look away from his intimate gaze, down at the gauze covering the puncture wounds on his neck. "What got you out there?"

He says it so simply: "You know that story about fang baby off Old Pearsall?"

My eyes bug out of their sockets. "I'm not fucking playing—"

"Neither am I!"

Glaring at him, I say loudly, "Vampires aren't real. That's just an old urban legend to scare kids into staying at home after dark."

"Just like la lechuza?"

I scrub a hand over my face. "Zakary, I swear to fuckin' God... Old Pearsall is, like, fifteen miles away, for Christ's sake!"

"Yeah, well, guess it went out for a night drive or fly or whatever vampires do."

"You're a big dude. How the hell could a baby attack you?"

He shrugs. "I've had a lot to drink."

I throw my hands in the air when he reaches for the glass half-full of amaretto. "Maybe you should lay off the fuckin' bottle, huh?"

He scoffs, returning the glare. "Don't you think you showin' up out of nowhere's got me fucked up? Huh?"

A baby cries at the door.

The hair on the back of my neck stands at attention.

"Did you make a deal with the devil?" I whisper.

The air is eerily still, the whole house gone too quiet. Zak refuses to look at me, nor does he answer.

I take the glass from his hand and down the rest of the amaretto, shifting my weight uncomfortably. "Does Adrian know? About—" I gesture toward the front of the house, "—Kris being on her lechuza bullshit tonight?"

Zak nods once. "I told him to stay away." Then, he sighs. "I cussed at her and threw salt out the door, but we're gonna have to wait it out till morning."

Scoffing, I mutter, "Bitch hates me that much, I guess."

With Kris scratching at the door and crying, the scent of Adrian's soap lingering on my skin and Zak's clothing hanging from my frame, the realization sets in.

This is hell. And I'm in for a long fucking night.

Pursing my lips, I reach for my phone to text Mom so she doesn't freak out on me like she did this morning.

> Spending the night at a friends, had too much to drink. Sorry for bailing but I promise I'll be back tomorrow.

"Fuck," I grumble under my breath. I better be back tomorrow. If Kris somehow manages to eat me before sunrise, I'm going to be *so* pissed.

"I'm sorry about all this."

"Zak," I sigh, setting the drink and my phone down on the counter and facing him fully.

Everything finally hits me all at once, everything from what's happened tonight to what happened at New Year's Ball, violently colliding into my back and pushing me forward.

My arms slip around Zak's waist, and I lay my head on his chest. My eyes squeeze shut and I sniffle. "What if something really bad happened tonight, Z?"

He breathes in deeply before his arms envelop me. He mumbles into my hair, "I'm fine, babe. I promise."

I lift my head to search his face, to make sure he's not lying through his teeth to me. Not about this.

"What if I lost you for good, and—and I couldn't ever hear your voice again, or—" I grip him more tightly, my own voice rising higher as I blink rapidly, "—or see you play guitar again, or... or..."

I sob into his chest, gasping deeply.

I don't think I can say the rest of it.

After all this time, after reliving the same nightmare over and over every single night and coming home for this very reason, I don't know if I can say those words to Zak.

I don't deserve...

He takes my face between his hands and gently kisses my forehead. His lips linger, and my face crumples.

"Steph, I'm right here. I'm okay. I'm just drunk with a tiny flesh wound." He pulls away far enough to get a good look at me. The corners of his lips turn slightly upward.

Even the smallest smile of his has always taken my breath away.

"I'm more worried about you, mamas," Zak murmurs. "So let me do the limpia."

My eyes roll. "Scared I'll carry some bad juju from la lechuza?"

His expression falls somber. "Steph, I have to do it, or you might die."

I scoff incredulously and step back, making our arms drop from around one another. "Yeah right—"

"I'm not gonna let you fuck around and find out with this," he mutters, spinning around.

"Okay, riddle me this, Einstein," I start and follow him. I swipe away lingering trails of tears from my cheeks. "Why aren't *you* dying from blood loss and those puncture wounds, but if I don't do a limpia, I'll die? How the fuck does that make sense?"

"That's the legend, Steph," he says simply, opening a cabinet and reaching for an egg carton. "People who've been attacked by la lechuza die within a few days." He takes a single white egg out and sets the carton on the counter. "It's gotta be more than just a wound getting infected."

Zak frantically looks around, searching through cabinets.

"Ugh, fine. I'll do it if it'll make you feel better. But I want you to tell me the truth."

Looks like he might've found what he was looking for in another cabinet: a bottle of holy water. "'Bout what?"

"About what attacked you." I swallow the rock forming in my throat. "Why you missed the show tonight."

He gulps more amaretto. "I've been at the bar all afternoon. I drank enough that I didn't realize what time it was, and, by then, it was too late.

"So I was headin' home from the bar, and I saw a toddler playing on the bridge. I kinda freaked out and scooped it up before it fell into the river, and..." He blinks, staring off into space. "Fucker bit me."

I know he feels my eyes on him, but he avoids my gaze by reaching for a bottle from the cabinet.

It's bad enough for him to finally pull out his Crown Royal.

"You didn't make a deal with the devil to turn into a vampire, did you?" I joke, trying to lighten the mood.

He groans and rolls his eyes. He doesn't even bother with a glass, unscrewing the Crown and taking a swig straight from the bottle.

My stomach sinks so low that I think I'm going to puke. "Z, what did you do?"

He finally snaps, "I made a deal with the devil for my fucking life, okay?"

CHAPTER 18

60CM OF STEEL

–ALPHA WOLF FT. HOLDING ABSENCE

I STARE AT ZAK FOR THE LONGEST MOMENT, GAPING at him like he just grew two extra heads and started speaking Chinese.

First, his sister is la lechuza.

Second, he was bit by fang baby.

Third… "You made a deal with the devil for your life?"

"Babe, I…" Zak's face twists and contorts, stammering.

I stare at the gauze covering his neck. When I blink, I can still see his neck covered in blood and rain. "You lost so much blood."

"Yeah," he agrees, almost laughing with a crazed look on his face. "Yeah, I lost *too* much blood."

My eyes sting. "You should be dead right now," I whisper. A violent tempest churns in my abdomen and threatens to come out either as vomit or uncontrollable sobs.

Zak sucks his bare bottom lip between his teeth, face still contorting until it settles on an emotion: pain.

"That thing wouldn't let me go," he says softly. "When it finally did, I was barely awake. My—" his hand covers his chest, "—my heart, I couldn't really feel it beating anymore. It's so hot outside, but-but I was so cold. And…"

His throat bobs as he looks away. "That's when I saw him. Barely. I couldn't feel anything, I couldn't really see, but I could smell rotten eggs.

"He asked if I wanted to live. When I said yes, it's like lightning hit my chest," he explains, striking his chest with a fist, "and it felt like I breathed for the first time. Then… he was gone. And that's when I realized you were on the side of the road yelling at me."

"What's the rest of it?" I demand. "You made a deal. Your life for what?"

Zak swallows, his lips parting as he searches my eyes.

But nothing comes out.

He shakes himself out of it before lifting up the egg. "I gotta do this."

When I don't start arguing, he takes the holy water and splashes some over the egg, making a sign of the cross over it while muttering, "En el nombre del Padre, y del Hijo, y del Espiritu Santo. Amen."

He's about to touch the top of my head with the egg, but I gently grab his wrist.

"Babe—"

"Is that really why you bailed tonight? You were nervous?"

He tries to pull away. "I gotta do this."

But my grip tightens. "Not until you tell me why I filled in for your sorry ass at the show even though you asked me to come."

Zak's hand finally falls. His face contorts in disbelief. "You… you *played?*"

"Don't play dumb with me. I know y'all set me up."

Zak shakes his head vehemently, shushing me and insisting, "No, no, we didn't. I swear."

"Well, it sure as shit seems like it!" I screech. "What the hell is going on, Zak? Because, apparently, your sister is la lechuza, and you've been attacked by a vampire baby and made a deal with the devil to live to see another day, so you and Adrian setting me up tonight is definitely within the realm of possibilities tonight!"

"What does it matter?" he says before taking a nip of Crown.

My jaw drops. "Excuse me?"

He grins. One of his teeth glints a little. "I'm drunk, remember?"

I glare at him for a solid moment until he starts giggling. I smack his shoulder with my good arm. "You think Kris is wearing a chancla on her talons I can borrow to hit you with? I am so fucking sick of you Ramos twins already. Fuck."

Zak chuckles still, sipping and gazing at me with amusement lighting up his honey-brown eyes. "Ay, mamas. I might like that."

I try to bite back uncomfortable laughter, but it slips.

Despite la lechuza—Kris freaking Ramos-Dempster the owl-witch man-eater, herself—scratching at the door and forcing me to spend the night with my ex-boyfriend who supposedly made a deal with the devil to live after being attacked by a vampire baby... this feels normal.

Sharing an awkward, flirtatious laugh with Zak is remarkably normal and deliciously familiar.

Zak hands me the glass with a drunken simper. "Drink up. Your ex is about to feel you up under the guise of limpia."

I choke. "Don't you *ever* say that combination of words ever again." I add under my breath, "Bet you won't be limp after it, either."

That sends Zak reeling, snorting and bent over laughing.

The faint sound of an egg cracking makes him gasp. "Oh,

shit," he cackles, looking stupefied at the egg covering his hand and the counter.

The yolk falls to the floor, landing the same time thunder claps.

Guffawing, I nudge him aside and reach for paper towels. "It's bedtime, drunk ass. I'm not letting you baptize me in egg yolk."

Zak doesn't argue, only washes his hands. When I turn around after tossing spoiled paper towels, I find him watching me intently, the same way he would during a practice or jam session when we were coming up with something new. "What was it like bein' back on stage?"

My expression slowly falls, and nostalgia smothers my chest. It takes a moment, but I say in a soft murmur, "I missed it so fucking much."

I don't have to look to know he's smirking.

"It's different without you up there."

The bottle of Crown on the counter is far too enticing as he echoes his twin's sentiments.

He rubs his bearded chin. "It really hasn't been the same since you left."

I really don't want to talk about this. And, yet, just like earlier today, I can't help but spill my fucking guts to Zak.

"I haven't even picked up a guitar since that NYB concert. I haven't played guitar in so long, and—" my fingers flex, balling up and stretching out in front of me, "—somehow, these damn things remember every single note. Like I went on an extra-long vacation and just needed a little warm up to get back into it."

The tense silence returns, descending into the kitchen between us like a suffocating fog. It's like this fucking night won't come to an end.

"Why'd you completely give up music?" he asks. "It doesn't make sense for you to give it up."

I grimace, my stomach churning. I never wanted to admit this to anyone, but Zak's always had a way of pulling things out of me. It wasn't until I was hundreds of miles away and deleted his number and socials that I could finally cut myself off from telling him everything.

"Playing outside of Timeless didn't make sense to me," I admit. "I don't care how good of a guitarist I am. Outside of Timeless, guitar doesn't make sense to me. Music doesn't make sense." My heart sinks deep in my chest, threatening to plummet into my stomach. "Nothing really made sense after I left."

"Yeah," he murmurs softly. "I get that."

Above the rain, a distinct *tap, tap, tap* against glass behind me sends ice knifing straight into my spine. My entire body seizes.

I start to turn, but Zak grabs me and forces my face into his chest.

"Don't look," he murmurs into my hair. "Go to the back of the house and don't look outside. I'll handle this."

"Are you sure?" I whisper. "You're still drunk."

The tapping becomes louder, more pronounced.

Zak squeezes me tighter when I wince. "I got it, babe. Go. And do *not* look back."

He releases his grip around me and pushes me out of the kitchen.

I run as soon as Zak starts yelling. "Vamos, pendeja! Fuck off!"

Without even thinking about it, I make a dash for Zak's room.

Chapter 19

Dial Tone

–Catch Your Breath

ZAK YELLS AN ASSORTMENT OF CURSES AT HIS sister screeching outside the kitchen window, some in English, but mostly in Spanish, a lot of which leaves me wondering what the hell he just said since I don't recognize the words.

I flinch and stop pacing when my phone dings in the pocket of Zak's shorts hanging from my hips.

U find Z?

Yeah and now I wish I didn't.

"God, she is not giving up tonight."

My feet lift off the ground at the sound of Zak's voice behind me. I spin around to face him, wide-eyed with hair standing straight up on the back of my neck.

"Sorry," he mumbles.

My phone dings again.

Y what happened??

I stare at the dimly lit screen, wondering. "Does Brandy or Robbie or anyone else know about Kris?" I ask.

"No," he responds quickly in a loaded, firm voice. "Only Shannon. And it's best they don't, okay?"

I nod before texting Robbie back.

> Just another night of being a sad drunk.

At least I'm not lying to him as Zak passes by with the Crown in hand.

"Haven't you had enough to drink yet?"

He walks all the way to the opposite side of the bed and sets the bottle on a nightstand before flopping onto the mattress with a heavy sigh. "I think tonight's a special occasion and I can have a little more."

"As long as you share."

Zak smirks, grabbing the bottle and unscrewing the cap. "Desperate much?"

He sips directly from the bottle before holding it out in my direction across the empty side of the bed between us.

I'm still leaning against the charcoal wall with an eyebrow arched at him.

He cocks his head. "You gonna stand there all night?"

I shrug. "Figured you hate me enough to not want me near you ever again."

Zak's gaze softens. "I don't hate you."

The admission leaves me stunned. I'd take a step back from it if I wasn't already on the wall.

Eventually, I move forward and climb onto the bed beside him. I sit crossed-legged and take the Crown, the stuff burning my throat on its way down.

"I'm stuck with my ex-boyfriend for a night after refusing his proposal, not talking to him for a year and a half, and him miraculously surviving death," I mutter. "Which, by the way, I expect the real story tomorrow when you're sober."

Zak titters, crossing his arms. He pushes his back against the headboard. "Are you really gonna have an aunty date with Drea?" he asks.

"Yeah, of course I am. I mean, as long as Kris doesn't try to fuckin' murder me."

"Just don't want la princesita's heart getting broken again with you disappearing."

Drea's, or yours?, I want to ask. "I'm not going anywhere. I'm gonna make good on my promise to her."

He pauses, chewing on his lip and mulling something over silently for a long moment. "Since Kris is a little off the deep end for the time being, I can get her and y'all can hang out here."

Leaning back against the headboard next to Zak, I slap his arm with the back of my hand and point at him. "No tios allowed."

"We turned her old room into a playroom-slash-study room for her, and no tios are allowed in there." When his mouth spreads wide, I catch a glimpse of an open-faced gold cap on his incisor. "Not unless they bring snacks."

I smile over at Zak warmly. My stomach flutters when he returns it.

"How come you haven't settled down with a nice girl and started your own brood? You'd make a wonderful daddy."

His cheerfulness falters. "I tried that a couple years ago. Kinda backfired."

I have to look away, at anything in the opposite direction. "I said a nice girl," I smart under my breath. It hitches before I can muster the next question. "You haven't dated since?"

He hesitates. "No."

I have to clear the sudden thickness in my throat. "Your last girl sounds like a bitch."

"Yeah," he sighs, letting his head fall back against the wall with a *thud*. "But I love her." He snorts. "Guess I get why Shannon handled things the way he did."

My throat seizes, and I stop breathing. I make myself sip more Crown to burn all the emotions threatening to project all over myself and the fucking floor.

But it's too late.

"I don't know how I could go on if tonight was your last."

Zak's head lifts in my periphery. "You left me without telling me why. Hell, you never even actually broke up with me—you just said you quit the band, left town, and didn't return my calls or texts. Why would things change now if I died?"

"Because it'd mean I'd never have the chance to apologize," I whisper as I stare at the dark bedspread.

Zak pauses, taking the Crown from my hand and taking the longest gulp. A cap screws, and glass slides over wood, but he stays silent.

I glance over my shoulder, finding him watching me.

His brows raise, and so does his hand. "Well?"

Turning away, my tongue wets my bottom lip. "I'm sorry, Z. I'm sorry for embarrassing you and running. For cutting you out the way I did and not answering when you called."

Fat, hot tears roll down my cheeks, and my lip trembles as I force the courage to confess up from my gullet. With it comes a gut-wrenching sob that shakes me, but I make myself turn to face the one I never should've wronged, ever.

I might be a goddamn coward, but I owe him this much. I owe looking him in the eye and admitting how much I fucked up.

Zak's heartbreak forming on his face all over again blurs, worsening as I try to blink away the tears.

"I'm so sorry I cheated on you," I finally blubber. "I got

too drunk and too high, and I regret every bit of it. I regret leaving. I regret everything."

Unconsolable sobs consume the bedroom, and I hide my heated face behind trembling hands. I knew apologizing wasn't going to be easy, but I didn't expect it to stem from the terror of possibly losing Zak for good, either.

A warm hand covers my knee.

My hands shake as I dash away tears, sniffling and trying to blink away more tears coming. "I don't expect you to forgive me—"

"I don't," he cuts me off with an edge in his tone. "I don't forgive you."

Something inside me snaps, transforming sniveling into worsening sobs.

I know I've hurt Zak beyond repair—I've known that since the moment I woke up in the back of the Suburban with Adrian's arms still firmly planted around me—but being here in the flesh, confirming it beyond a shadow of a doubt, has me wishing I could fall off the face of the earth into a black hole.

"I never thought you'd admit it to me," Zak says quietly.

Gasping, I rub his shirt I'm wearing over my face to dry the tears. "I—I came back to apologize. I couldn't stop seeing your face every night I was gone, and I miss home, I miss NYB, Timeless, and—"

I stop myself before I let everything out, hiccuping at the sudden cease and desist like my body took a moment to catch up with my brain.

I miss you, Chiquito.

Zak rubs his thumb across my knee. He stares off into space, the corners of his mouth turned so, so slightly upward. Eventually, his head rolls over. He doesn't say anything for a long moment, just contemplates me wiping streams of tears away. "Everyone misses you, too."

"Everyone?"

"Yeah, even my sorry ass." He reaches for my hand and squeezes it gently. "I never wanted you to go, Steph."

The scoff that passes my lips is visceral. "God, you're so fucking drunk—"

Zak reaches for my face, hand caressing my cheek, and *he kisses me*.

I immediately push him away. "What the hell are you doing?"

"If tonight was my last, you'd regret not apologizing," Zak murmurs. His eyes flash to my mouth. "And I'd regret not kissing you again. Just one last time."

We stare at one another, my breathing hard and heavy and in disbelief.

His gaze is hypnotic until it's too late: Zak's warm lips are on mine again.

I moan as my fingers curl in his thick hair. His brawny arm slips around my waist to draw me closer.

Being so close to him stokes a furious fire in my core, blistering everything until I press my lips against his again like it's the only thing that can tame the flames.

"I'm so sorry, Z," I murmur breathlessly.

His lips travel from my shoulder to my neck. My eyes close when he plants a wet kiss on my throat.

"I don't deserve it, but I hope you forgive me one day."

He takes my chin and silences me by locking his mouth to mine.

Beyond the burn of liquor lingering on his tongue, beyond the new muscles and tattoos and shiny hardware, beyond the feigned machismo, everything about Zak is exactly how I left him.

He still smells like cedar and vetiver beneath the whisky. He still holds me just right, his strong arms locking all the fallen pieces back into place where they belong.

He still tastes like home.

Zak's tongue runs over my neck, tasting my flesh. The bolt in his tongue sends a pleasant shiver down my spine.

With my hand at the back of his head, I pull him even closer.

He tears away. "Get out."

"What?" I ask breathlessly.

His heat disappears, and he sits on the edge of the bed. "Get out."

Slowly, I sit up, studying the gray shirt on his back facing me. "Did I—"

"I said get out."

My bottom lip trembles as it juts out. I can't pry my gaze from Zak, but I force myself up from his bed and out of his room.

Slamming the door, the ache in my chest finally breaks me.

I really thought there was something there. I thought... I thought...

My face crumples, and I turn to leave until I glance down and realize I'm still wearing his stupid clothes. I strip them off as quickly as I can, throwing them at his door, before running down the hallway to put distance between us.

I don't know what I was thinking.

Zak is drunk. He's nostalgic and hates me for what I did to him.

There's no way he will ever forgive me.

But as I rush through the house, capturing a glimpse of something large and white in the darkened kitchen window in my periphery, I remember just how fucked I am tonight. I'm still imprisoned in this house and hiding from la lechuza, the only thing I can for sure confirm is real and true tonight.

Everything else... who fucking knows.

I should sleep on the couch, but the thought of being any

closer to Zak than I need to be sends angry tears surging over the brim of my waterline. So I slam Adrian's bedroom door behind me.

Zak shouldn't want me, anyway. I broke his heart and shouldn't be forgiven for it. Not with what I did.

I raid Adrian's drawers after turning a lamp on and find an old, oversized Timeless tee. I start to shut the drawer until a glimmering plastic package catches my attention.

Reaching for and examining it in what little light the lamp gives off, it's a set of black candles.

A crease forms between my brows. I glance down in the drawer to see if anything is underneath, then around his room to check for any candles not on the bookshelves.

Shutting the drawers, something rattles on top before rolling. It heads for the floor until I catch it.

White chalk.

I groan underneath my breath as I replace it on top of the dresser, keeping an eye on it as I pull the shirt on.

Figures, Adrian's calling on the devil and making sacrifices, yet Zak's the one sealing a deal for his life.

That is, if his drunk ass isn't exaggerating.

I settle into Adrian's bed like I own the damn room. Like I belong here. All while Zak is on the other side of the house probably laughing to himself.

Tears fill my eyes as I curl up into a ball under the sheets. A sudden sob scares a hiccup out of me.

It feels like my heart is splitting in two, cracking wide open what I thought I cemented back together and shoved under a dark and dusty bed to be forgotten about.

My vision clouds over before I bury my face into Adrian's pillow.

CHAPTER 20

THE WAY YOU LIKE IT

–ADEMA

SOMETHING BRUSHES ALONG MY FACE AND JOLTS me awake. My eyes snap wide open until bright light blinds me and has me rubbing my eyes, before my vision refocuses.

Adrian watches me.

"Hey, baby. Good morning," he greets softly. His fingertips trace my cheek. "Nice comin' home to you in my bed."

"What the fuck," I groan in a whisper. Then, my head snaps up sharply.

Kris.

Zak.

The show.

Adrian watching me with a small smirk, beside me in his bed.

I drag a hand over my face. "Shit."

He chuckles, brushing hair off my shoulder. "I always thought you were cute when you're asleep."

Ignoring the comment, I ask in a voice hushed from hoarseness, "Is Kris gone yet?"

This is what I get for filling in for Zak at the concert and not being properly warmed up.

"Yeah." He glances at the window illuminated with morning light that glints off his nose ring. "She always goes home before sunrise."

Adrian's gaze lingers on the window, the sunlight giving his features a soft glow and highlighting the honey color in his brown eyes. His hair is damp and combed, and the scent of his woody soap is strong on his skin. Even his face is freshly shaven. He's shirtless because of course he is.

A smirk tugs at the corner of his mouth. "Maybe next time you come to a show you should warm up."

I whack his thigh and he jumps. "There ain't gonna be a next time."

"Mm, sure." He turns toward his nightstand, reaching for something, and brings a colorful mosaic mug into view. "You still like your coffee dark and sweet?"

I'm careful to keep my lower half covered and not bump into the coffee as I sit up. "Um, yeah," I say, taking the mug from him with furrowed brows. "Thanks, I guess."

I stifle a groan when I take a sip and it tastes like perfection.

Son of a bitch.

Clearing my throat, I ask, "Is Zak okay?"

"He's fine. Even went to Mass."

Of course the good Catholic boy did. "Did he tell you what happened?"

"Mhmm." Weight shifts beside me, making the bed creak. Adrian's fingers trace the bandage on my arm before leading it to his lips to kiss just above the gauze. "You shouldn't have left the gig last night."

I hone in on the white chalk on Adrian's dresser. I chew my lip and mull the thought over in my head for a long moment before voicing it. "You're the one behind the shit going on at the bridge."

He hums against my shoulder. "No."

My brows knit together as I turn to look at him. "Then what the hell are the chalk and black candles for? It's the same shit on the bridge."

"You're kidding, right? How many other people in Bexar County have chalk and black candles, you think? I co-own a botanica, for Christ's sake." He taps my arm. "Maybe *you're* the one behind the bridge since you're the one finding shit, huh?"

Something still isn't adding up. "Why didn't you want me to find Zak last night?"

Adrian's arm slips under mine, wrapping around my waist to draw me closer. "I wanted you to myself. You were incredible at the show."

His nose skims the column of my neck up to my ear, and his hand slips beneath his shirt I'm wearing. His breath hitches as his calloused hands search for bottoms or underwear over my hip but find none.

"Oh." His lips press against my neck. "You wanna make up for it, huh?"

I push him away and climb out of bed, keeping my lower bits covered by yanking the T-shirt down while balancing coffee in hand. I think I left my clothes in his bathroom. "Abso-fucking-lutely not."

His low chuckle follows me as I grab my phone from the nightstand and head out of the bedroom.

Ty's name greets me with a new message.

> You back in Timeless without telling me?

> No. Just covered for Zak since he was out sick.

The perfect cup of coffee mocks me on the bathroom counter as I search for an extra toothbrush.

My phone buzzes.

> Yeah sure. Covering code for y'all seeing how it goes over with fans before pulling the trigger?

"Okay, motherfucker," I grumble aloud as I toss my phone aside. I'm not going to answer him if he's going to be an asshole like that.

A cool splash of water soothes my puffy skin and swollen eyes, but it doesn't touch my flaring temper when I stare at the coffee as I pat my face dry. Adrian might be happy about having me to himself this morning, but he still has a lot to answer for from last night.

I just hate that the coffee hits the spot so perfectly as I make my way down the hall, where I find him cutting up fruit in the kitchen.

He perks up like an excited puppy when he sees me. "More coffee?"

I make a point of setting my mug in the sink. "No."

"Breakfast?"

"No."

"A swift kick in the ass?"

I cross my arms, and he laughs as he tosses fruit into a bowl.

As expected, he tops the strawberries and pineapple chunks with plenty of Tajín. "I feel you staring at me."

"Did y'all set me up last night?" I demand.

"For what?"

"For me to fill in for Zak at the show."

Adrian cocks his head as he chews. "Guess you didn't see me calling his sorry ass multiple times to see where the fuck he was."

"I'm not gonna ask to get back into the band."

"No," he says through a mouthful, "you're gonna fuckin' beg."

My jaw drops. "Excuse you?"

"Zak wasn't the only one hurt when you left. La princesita cried for weeks. Shannon hasn't been the same. Robbie went off the deep end." He goes silent for a moment, staring at the counter with hardened eyes. "It tore me up, too. Timeless shuttered after you left. We came—" he pinches his index finger and thumb almost together, "—this close to calling it quits. But we've tried to make it work."

I throw my hands in the air. "Last I checked, Timeless has put out another album, gone on tour, and gotten even bigger. Y'all have been doing pretty fuckin' well without me."

Adrian sets his breakfast down on the counter. "Yeah, and I don't know if you've noticed, but we've finally hit the wall, Steph. It's the end. All because you decided you'd rather ghost everyone than own up to your fucking mistake."

I scowl at him. "It was your mistake as much as it was mine."

He steps closer and his gaze softens. "Yeah," he murmurs, "and I wanted to work things out. I still wanna work things out. With the band *and* with you."

"Why are you trying to make this—" I gesture between us, "—a thing?"

He makes a face. "'Cause we are 'a thing'."

My eyes nearly bug out of my head. "Are you fucking kidding me? You think I'm gonna want you after you cheated on your girlfriend? You think it's fine to not be faithful and fuck around when you're with someone?"

"The fuck do you call what you did to my brother, then?"

I could choke him. "The biggest mistake of my fucking life, that's what."

His lips purse. "I'm sorry for what I did to Norma and what we did to Zak. But I'm not letting you go again."

My face falls even further. "What part," I begin, stepping toward Adrian and shoving him, "of 'I fucking hate you' do you not get, asshole?"

He pushes my shoulder back. "Maybe I'm getting mixed signals with you fuckin' me, wearin' my clothes, and sleepin' in my bed."

My jaw drops, and I shove him even harder. "Ugh!"

Adrian pushes me again, sending me stumbling toward the wall. But I bounce back and race toward him.

Adrian catches my wrist before my palm meets his face. He twists my arm and pins it behind my back, propelling me into the counter. The quartz bites at my hips as his crotch grinds into my ass.

"Slap me again and see what happens, bitch."

I swing my leg around to trip him backwards. When his grip slips, I spin around to smack him across the face.

"Call me a bitch one more time," I say through gritted teeth.

An evil smirk tugs at the corner of his lips. "Bitch."

Lurching forward, my fingers knot in Adrian's hair to tilt his head back. I slap him again before he tackles me onto the floor.

He towers over me and his hand comes to my throat. "Fuck did I say about slappin' me, huh?" he seethes, pressing down on my neck.

I bust his cheek again.

Adrian pins both arms above my head onto the floor and grabs at my shorts. "This is what you want, isn't it?"

I wriggle and kick until he releases my hands, and I slap him as he snatches my shorts. "Get the fuck offa me!"

No matter how hard I hit him, Adrian still manages to rip my shorts and underwear off.

When he pauses to unbutton his black jeans, I scramble away.

Hands wrap around my ankles and yank me back. "Fuck you think you're goin'?"

I smack his chest before he shoves my legs apart and kneels between my thighs, letting his stiff dick settle in my slit and making all the warmth in my body drain to my pussy. He clamps my hands above my head before I can run.

Adrian's position sends a throbbing ache through me.

I'm not going to let him do this to me—I'm not going to let him win and beg for his cock to thrust all the way inside.

Adrian's tip slips a little, making my hands clench into fists so I don't rock my hips, or whimper, or close my eyes.

The smug look on his face says he knows I'm weak. "Just admit it, Steph," he purrs from above.

He moves his hips so slightly, and his cock slips a little further. My fingernails dig into my palms, but it still happens: my body flushes head to toe with heat and desire. My eyelids close, and I bite my bottom lip.

"Just admit that you want me," he says in my ear with a low, raspy voice.

"You're a piece of shit," I grit out, more of a reminder to myself to do the right thing and not give in.

"So are you, fuckin' slut."

I snatch my wrists free, and Adrian topples over before I can escape. I push him off and scramble up from the floor.

Eyeballing my underwear next to him, Adrian is quick to kick them and my shorts away.

His eyes narrow, summing me up half-naked before him. "I like it better when you're only wearing one of my shirts."

I scoff. "I don't give a shit what you like."

His hand flashes under my chin, grasping my throat and shoving me against the nearest wall. "Fine."

Adrian positions himself between my lower lips, sighing as he slips and slides through the wetness that's been building between my legs. My eyes flutter closed, savoring the throbbing heat moving under me and against my clit, before realizing he's staring right at me.

He presses his lips against mine and murmurs, "I'll do what you like, then."

CHAPTER 21

THE DRUG I NEED

–AGAINST ALL WILL

I SIGH SOFTLY WHEN THE SWOLLEN HEAD OF Adrian's dick ridges over my clit. Gulping down air doesn't help make sense of any of the scrambled thoughts in my head. "And what is it you think I like?"

"Just listen to you," Adrian says softly. He leans in close, his hips bumping into mine as he draws his flattened tongue up my neck. His movements pulsate, and he kisses me long and hard as he groans softly with me.

He breaks away, murmuring, "Look at you." He pulls out almost all the way, just the tip lingering over my clit, and glances down.

When I follow his line of sight, he's literally dripping wet.

He drives his pelvis forward with a gentle grunt. "Face it, princesa," Adrian says lowly in my ear. "You like anything I do to you." His fingers tighten around my throat, and he nibbles the electrified skin beneath my ear. "And you're gonna keep crawling back for more 'cause you're a fucking whore for me."

My eyes flutter closed as more wetness floods over his

cock. I bite back a whimper, letting out a soft sigh as my fingernails dig into his hips colliding with mine.

It doesn't go unnoticed.

He lifts me up by the ass and nails my soaking wet pussy to the wall. The groans in my ear are hardly audible with blood rushing through my ears.

Teeth scrape over the flesh of my neck, and he thrusts harder.

My eyes roll back and soft cries permeate the kitchen, relishing his complete attention, his obsession with me. My inner walls clench tightly around his cock, begging to be obliterated.

He feels way too damn good.

"What about a condom?"

Adrian kisses me roughly, groaning as he drills deeper. "I'll come in you if I want to," he mumbles against my lips.

"What if *I* don't want you to?"

"I'm a piece of shit, remember?" His head tilts back, exposing his tattooed neck. "What do I care what you want?"

Hypnotized by his stupid throat, I pull him closer to press my mouth against his flesh. "I don't want to get pregnant, asshole."

He chuckles lowly. "What, you're the one good Catholic girl not on birth control?"

I grab his jaw and force him to look at me. "I don't want you to come in me, fuckhead."

Adrian's pupils expand before he carries me to the counter. The second he sets me down, his sweet and spicy mouth smashes onto mine and he pistons hard and fast, relentlessly chasing his pleasure.

I let him part my lips—I want to taste him just this once where neither of us are fucked up, when it's daylight and I don't exactly have to hide my shame.

He fills me completely, grinding until I whimper for more and pull him closer with my legs wrapped around his waist. My fingers fan out in his thick, damp hair, and I pant over his lips when his hips pound into me. A deluge of pleasure undulates through my core.

His gaze sets me more on edge than I actually am on the counter. "If you don't stop that, you're gonna make me come," he rasps.

Reluctantly, my legs release the death grip around his waist, spreading wide. My hand slips between us and slinks down to roughly play with my clit. "Oh, God, Adrian," I whine.

The rhythmic smacking of wet skin suddenly stops when he pulls out and pumps his cock by hand over mine, grunting and gasping. The whimper that falls out of me is so fucking desperate as Adrian comes on my hand furiously circling my clit.

Thick, hot come dribbles down my fingers, his lusty moans resounding in my ears.

My eyes roll to the back of my head and thighs snap together as a jolt splits up my spine. It threatens to tear me apart and completely unravel me before Adrian on the kitchen counter like a goddamn buffet for him to devour.

He's always made me do stupid shit. Right now is no different as he watches me bring my hand to my mouth to lick our collective come off my fingers.

He sputters, propping himself up on his hand that rests beside my hip on the counter as he leans over me, spent.

I swipe a come-soaked finger across his lips. His tongue darts out to wrap around and draw it into his mouth, moaning softly as he consumes our pleasure in a perverse communion.

When my fingers fall from his lips, he dives in for a deep,

dangerous, sloppy, and sex-flavored kiss that makes my hips jerk, already begging to be filled again.

"Swear to fuckin' God, I'm gonna come inside you next time."

My head lulls back, relishing the aftershocks of pleasure still pulsing all the way to my curled toes. "Who said there's gonna be a next time?"

Adrian grabs the hair on the back of my head, making me gasp as he forces me to look up at him.

"Me."

He bends down to kiss me as roughly as he fucked me here on the counter. A lingering wave of pleasure flows from my mouth to my core.

Adrian pulls back, eyes searching. "I said you're mine." He kisses me once more. "I've waited long enough."

I turn away, scoffing and moving to wash my hands. "What part of 'no' do you not get, dude?"

Adrian comes up behind me, resting his hands on my hips as he leans down to press his mouth to my neck. "We're both finally single at the same time—'no' ain't an option, princesa."

My jaw drops and brows knit together when I spin around.

That's it. I'm gonna kill him.

I push Adrian away so I can pull on my shorts. "Us being together ain't an option either, wiseass."

He zips up his pants. "You wanna talk about me being better than fuckin' around when I'm with someone, but you're the only one I keep fuckin' around with. And as far as I know, I'm the only one you keep fuckin' around with, too."

"And if you're not?" I smart with fists resting on my hips.

Jealousy flares in his eyes as his jaw twitches. "You bringin' something back from Atlanta?"

I turn on my heel and head for the front door. "None of your fuckin' business, dude."

Adrian grabs my arm and snatches me back. "*You* are my business," he says lowly. "Keep pushing me away, and I'll keep fighting back."

I try to move away. "Us dating is a terrible idea that should never happen."

He forces me to turn and face him. "Why do you keep comin' around, then, huh?" he demands. "Why do you keep fuckin' me?"

I wrench my arm free from his grip. "You ever think the sex is good? Dree—" I swear all the hardness in his eyes melts away as I call him by his nickname for the first time in so long, "—even us being 'just friends' has been toxic. Neither of us have proven we're decent people. I don't see how anything could go right if we got together."

Moving to grab the doorknob, Adrian calls out, "You ever think nothing's been right because we've never given things between us a shot? A real one?"

I raise an eyebrow and take a deep breath before angling around. "What d'you mean?"

I'm used to Adrian being the cocky asshole who thinks his shit don't stink, but the guy before me now is desperate.

Enamored.

"You keep coming back to me, Steph. I—let's—" he stammers, searching for words. He closes his eyes and takes a deep breath before uttering, "Let me take you out on a date. A real date. And-and if things don't work out from there, then fine. But at least give me a fair shot. We've been bullshitting this long enough that we owe each other that much."

As much as I hate it, Adrian has a point. I left because of him. And now I'm home, I've come back to him. *Twice.*

I finally did the impossible last night and apologized to Zak. I came clean, admitted my wrongdoing to his face, and, hell, I even picked him up from the goddamn bridge and saved his ass from things getting any worse out there, twice, too.

What I did was unforgivable, though, and he's made it clear he won't forgive me.

It's slight, but I finally nod. "Okay." I point a finger at him. "But you're not tellin' a soul about this, you hear me?"

He raises his hands in surrender. "You got it, boss."

His tattooed hands fall to his sides, and that's when I notice the large white stain encompassing the entirety of his crotch.

I snort, hiding a smile behind my hand. "You, uh, you should change."

Adrian looks down and chuckles. His eyes are bright on me as I back away a couple of steps before heading outside.

"Tonight, then?"

Hot gusts of wind push me back and forth as I face Adrian. The bright sun has already made any trace of rain from last night disappear, but the humidity still boils up from the earth and leaves a thin film of ick covering my skin. "Tonight, what?"

"Let's go out tonight. I won't pick you up, if you don't want me to. But let's go out."

I start to roll my eyes and huff, but Adrian continues, "Look at it as getting it out of the way, if you want, alright?"

Mouth pinching to the side, I sum Adrian up as he stands before me in his black jeans with a white stain on the crotch from us fucking. My eyelids linger on a close, relishing the orgasm that coursed through me so hard.

"Okay," I finally relent. "But you have to surprise me. And not with no goddamn Applebee's or some shit. A *real* date. Got it?"

Adrian flashes his pearly teeth. "Yes, ma'am."

I can't stand that he waits at the door, watching me get

into my car and drive away. Pretty sure that beam is stuck to his face now.

The road leading home comes up quickly. The slight curve partially blocking the bridge from view sends a weird chill down my spine and into my stomach, even though the heat in my car is baking me alive.

The cut on my arm throbs. Burns.

I pull off to the side of the road just across the way from the road home, staring at what little I can see of the bridge from here. The wound pulses and stings.

The thought of seeing Kris as la lechuza makes me try to swallow the drought suddenly forming in my mouth.

This cat ain't about to get killed by curiosity. So I start to turn down the road home.

The car lurches. The engine sputters and stalls before rubber even has a chance to touch the asphalt.

I stare at the dashboard in disbelief. "You've gotta be fuckin' kidding me."

Turning the ignition once, twice, and once again—because a third time's a charm, right?—the damn thing refuses to make any sound, mechanical or electric.

My car's totally fucking dead.

I fume and grumble in the direction of the bridge. Without even the slightest bit of AC, heat overwhelms the cabin and turns it into an oven. I swipe my keys and phone and climb out—at least home isn't too far away.

Slamming the door shut behind me, I wait for a truck to pass by before I cross the road. But it starts slowing down, and I recognize the driver and the passenger in the gun metal green GMC.

"Hey, sweet pea," Dad calls out when he rolls the window down. He throws his salt-and-pepper bearded chin toward my car. "You been keeping up with taking care of that?"

I grimace. Zak was always the one to take my car in for an

oil change and I... kinda dropped the ball on keeping up with it.

Dad tuts knowingly. "C'mon. I'll grab a chain from the house and we'll come back for it in a minute."

I sigh in relief and cross the street, opening the door behind Dad and hop inside a blissfully cool cabin.

Just to be greeted with Zak staring at me.

CHAPTER 22

THE ENEMY INSIDE

–DREAM THEATER

I FREEZE IN PLACE, DEBATING THE NEGATIVES OF walking five minutes in the heat and risking rattlesnake bites versus being stuck in a vehicle with my parents and my ex for one minute.

"Hurry up, you're letting the AC out," Mom complains.

Gnawing on my bottom lip, I plop down ungracefully inside the truck and shut the door, careful to stay as close to it as possible to avoid any and all contact with Zak even though this is a big truck and we wouldn't touch unless one of us reached over the console.

Dad glances in the rearview as he turns onto our road. "Missed you comin' to Mass with us, Steph."

"Sorry," I grumble.

"You're not missin' next week," Mom states. "You can get the partyin' outta your system before next weekend."

Thank God home isn't too far away. I flee the moment Dad parks, heading straight for the house.

"Z, you mind helpin' me get her car after breakfast?"

I spin around. "I'll help." My glare sets in on Zak as Dad passes by me. "You can go."

"And miss Mom's cookin'?" Zak says incredulously, following Dad. "Nah."

Without thinking, I reach out and grab Zak's wrist, yanking him back. My glower settles on his neck and the bandage replacing the gauze. At least he's not bleeding out over his navy button-down and dark jeans straining over his musculature.

The sun beams over his shoulder. "Guess you're not a vampire after all, huh?"

He forces a tight-lipped smile that spreads gold lip studs apart. "Guess not."

He tries making a move, but I pull him back. "What the *fuck* do you think you're doing?" I whisper furiously.

"What I've done almost every Sunday since you've been gone," he sneers, pulling away. "Having breakfast with your parents after church since you think you're too good for 'em."

I glare holes into his back before quickly catching up, shoving past him as I bite back, "So I guess sending flowers to your parents' graves even though I was hundreds of miles away don't count for shit, huh?"

His footsteps stop abruptly. He says so softly, "What?"

See what he thinks of me being too good now, I think as I let the door slam behind me. I might have left, but I never stopped caring, not even for Sunny and Lupe Ramos despite the fact they've been gone for almost eight years.

The door opens and Zak catches my arm before I have a chance to step inside the kitchen. He's careful of the cut as he makes me face him

If he doesn't stop looking at me like that…

"Why?" he demands quietly with an intense stare.

The smell of bacon frying and coffee brewing wafts in from the kitchen, like it's any normal Sunday.

He should know this by now, but maybe he doesn't. "Your

last girl might be a bitch and made some really bad decisions, but she still loves you," I utter before finally tearing myself away and storming into the kitchen.

I shouldn't have said that.

I should *not* have said that.

Especially not with him being under the same roof as my parents and having breakfast with them.

Especially when I just fucked his brother, *again*, right before I saw him.

"You missed another great Father Tomas homily today," Mom mentions as she pokes bacon in a pan. "He said he'd love to catch up with you after Mass next week."

Dad hands me a fresh mug of coffee and points to the sugar and creamer. Zak's eyes on me are like a fucking spotlight that burns the air, even when Dad hands him coffee.

Someone snaps their fingers repeatedly. "Hello, earth to Stephani!"

"Hmm?" I pull coffee away from my lips and looking at my mother. "I'm sorry, what?"

She glances at Dad and Zak heading to the dining room table before leaning in close. "I know this must be weird for you with Zak bein' here 'n' all, but he goes with us every Sunday when the band isn't out of town." She looks over at him. "I know it's because he misses his parents, but havin' him around has made it feel like you were a lot closer to home."

Gaping, it takes me a moment to remind her, "We broke up how long ago?"

She scowls. "Tsk, and y'all were inseparable for years before that."

I return her scowl. "I thought you were wise enough to know that people and relationships change."

Mom's lips purse as she flips bacon in the pan. "What happened to your arm?"

I hardly glance at it. "Accident."

She sucks in a sharp breath. "Heard you played at the show last night," she says a little too loudly.

Oh, this is going to be good.

"Yeah," I say, matching her volume. "Zak decided to bail and Adrian threw me under the bus to take his place."

The silence that cuts through the kitchen and dining room is so, so sweet.

Dad clears his throat. "Well, that's disappointing," he says.

I turn away from Mom to hide my satisfaction.

"But," he continues, "it seems like it might've worked in Timeless's favor."

That makes me spin around. "What?" I say the same time as Zak.

Dad smacks his lips after a sip of coffee and glimpses between us. "Word's gotten out about your appearance. I've started hearing some whispers through the grapevine there's renewed interest from a few labels."

I shrug and make a face. "So? What's that got to do with me?"

"Well, that's the thing," Dad says, shifting in his chair with his elbows on the table. "I think they'd offer a contract only if you return to the lineup."

I clench my jaw, ignoring Zak's obviously widened eyes. "Guess everyone's gonna be in a world of hurt, then."

"Maybe you should consider it," Dad says. He pauses. "That is, if the guys would want it."

All eyes are on Zak. His knuckles pale as he grips the mug between his hands and focuses on the tabletop. He doesn't say a word and doesn't look up at anyone or anything—his expression is indiscernible.

"*I* don't think it's a good idea," I say.

Mom suddenly spins around, letting a plate of bacon fall

ungracefully to the island counter and clatter. "What the hell happened to you two? Y'all were inseparable for years, and then—" She throws a hand in the air before it slaps against her leg and sets her glare on me, "—you randomly decided to quit the band and move out of state without any warning."

"Tara…"

Mom's glare shuts Dad right up before she sets in on me again. "Stephani, you're back home and you have a chance to come back to everything you left when you moved to Atlanta. Why wouldn't you take the chance?"

I gape at her with furrowed brows. "I'm not returning to Timeless," I state firmly. But my voice quivers, unintentionally going up half an octave and catching when I say, "Zak and I aren't getting back together."

A gigantic, jagged boulder forms in my throat and burns my nose. My fingers dig into the warm ceramic mug in my hand. I focus on the raw bacon sizzling and popping in the frying pan.

My shaky voice cracks. "He deserves better than me. And so does Timeless and everyone else."

Mom reaches for me, pulling me into a death grip of a hug. "Don't you dare think that for one second, sweetheart. We might be hurt about how you left, but every single one of us wants you here." She strokes my hair down my back and whispers, "Even Zak."

I blink rapidly, stunned, until I finally hug her back. My chest quivers from holding too much tension, and my throat is sore from swallowing knives.

A chair scrapes against the tile floor.

When I look up, Zak stalks out of the dining room, through the kitchen, and toward the front door. It slams shut a moment later.

The dam suddenly bursts.

I gently push Mom away and run for the backdoor.

He didn't want me to leave, but he doesn't want me back in the band.

Out on the back patio, I plant myself on a wooden bench in the shade. Renewed sobs fall out of me as quickly as the tears.

The door clicks and I throw my hands over my face to hide. But the second a hand touches my shoulder, I blubber everything out like uncontrollable vomit to get the illness out.

"I cheated on Zak," I finally blubber. "I thought I was doing everyone a favor leaving before I made things worse. But I miss home, and I miss the band, and—" I choke up. "I miss Zak."

Mom doesn't say a word, only holds me tight even though we're roasting out here in the heat and humidity with me making it worse by crying over us both.

Even though I'm admitting how much of a piece of shit I really am, I don't feel any better.

The more I admit it, the worse I feel.

Finally, after letting me sob on her shoulder for God knows how long, she says, "Well, that explains a couple of things."

Sniffling, I swipe my cheeks and titter brokenly. "You know what the awful thing is? Zak said he never wanted me to leave, even after I told him what I did. He..." My breath catches and tears fill my eyes again. I whisper so quietly that even I can't make it out over the screeching of cicadas. "He still loves me."

Mom squeezes my knee. "I can tell you still love him, too."

"But he doesn't forgive me," I tell her, finally meeting her gaze. "I don't blame him. I wouldn't forgive me, either." My head shakes. "I don't know what I expected."

She doesn't respond with anything for a minute, and it

sets me on edge. "Hon, what you did was beyond hurtful. It's hard to mend a relationship after trust is broken like that. But... it's not impossible. Might just take some extra time, if y'all are willing to work through it."

My lip trembles. "What if it doesn't work out?"

"All you can do is apologize, do better, and move on. Just because you messed up doesn't mean you stop living life to grovel for the rest of it."

My gaze goes soft on a cactus patch in the back corner of the yard that's baked under the sun for at least one hundred days too many.

I apologized; he made it clear that, even though there's still something between us, what I did was unforgivable. To be honest, I don't think I'd be able to forgive, either, no matter how much love I still might have afterward.

I wring my hands around my wrists. "I'm not sure what moving on looks like," I admit.

Mom pats my knee and kisses my head. "Whatever you want it to look like, baby." She rises from the bench and heads toward the door. "Biscuits should be ready in a few."

Taking a deep breath, I'm not sure what it is that I'm exhaling back into the Texas heat. It doesn't feel like relief, but, maybe, in some way, it is.

I'm not getting everything I had hoped for coming back, but I think I'm already getting so much more than what I deserve.

The gash on my arm suddenly stings, making me hiss and clutch at my arm. "Fuck," I groan, staring at the gauze that's now speckled with red.

Flicking at the tape, I gently peel it back.

The yowl that falls from my lips is like nails on a chalkboard at the sight of the pulsating gash swelling around the butterfly bandages and dripping with fresh blood. Bits of flesh have blackened, and small pockets of pus dot the cut.

I have to cover it up before I puke.

Swinging the door open, windows almost shatter as it hits the wall when I stumble into the kitchen. "Mom? Dad?"

Dad rushes back inside the kitchen. "What's wrong?"

"I... I need help."

Chapter 23

Adrenaline

−12 Stones

Peeling back the gauze, I show Dad the wound from la lechuza, the pus-filled and blackened rotting flesh that makes it look like my arm could fall off at any second.

He frowns, but he doesn't panic like I thought he would.

"How'd you cut yourself, sweetheart?" He gently handles my arm to further examine it. "Well, whatever you did here seems to be doing the trick. Just need a change of gauze, is all."

Following his line of sight, my brows furrow and lips part in confusion.

The gash on my arm is fine. No swelling around the butterfly bandages. No blackened flesh or pus. Just some fresh blood like I just stretched my arm too far and reopened part of the wound a little. "Oh."

"C'mon, sweet pea. I'll get you fixed up."

Dad leads me to the medicine cabinet in his and Mom's bathroom and replaces the gauze on my arm. Meanwhile, I stare at it like I just grew an extra limb—I *swear* it looked like it was about to fall off.

"You get this at the show last night?" Dad asks.

"Um, no," I say with a shake of my head. "Went a little too wild partying around mesquite afterwards, I guess."

Dad exhales through his teeth, that sound of a disappointed but understanding father. "Sounds like you need to settle down."

Slowly and wide-eyed, I nod. "Agreed."

After firmly taping the fresh gauze in place, Dad takes my hand and gives it a small squeeze. "You should think about it, Steph."

My head shakes and I whisper, "It's not a good idea."

"Would you do it if Zak wanted you back in the band?"

I don't look up from the floor. "There's still the *other* problem."

Dad pauses, leaning all his weight onto one foot. "Since when have you let boys get in the way of your dreams?"

I gape at him, trying to form some smart-ass remark, but nothing comes.

"Forget your dating life for a minute. Are you really gonna continue to sacrifice a solid music career over some mediocre lay?"

My jaw drops. "Dad!"

"What? I'm tellin' you like I tell any dude with girl problems. No matter how good the sex is, it's not worth your dreams and career. That usually lasts a lot longer than one night." He drops my hand and glances toward the door. "Don't you dare tell your mother what I said or she'll have us both in the confessional first thing tomorrow morning."

I scoff, crossing my arms and watching him leave. "Yeah, I'll keep your pep talk under wraps, old man."

It's quiet, but I hear Dad's snort before he turns the corner.

I chortle, too, until I glance down and spot fresh blood soaking the gauze.

No matter how many times I change the gauze, the blood seems to stay. And no matter how many times I have Mom and Dad both double check the wound on my arm, they insist it looks fine. Kind of deep, but still fine.

The only thing that gets my mind off the wound I definitely should've gone to the ER for, regardless if others say it's fine, is getting ready for my date with Adrian.

Even though I slip on a summer dress with off-the-shoulder sleeves long enough to cover the gauze, I find myself glancing down at my arm and wondering if it's going to fall off when I least expect it. Say, when I'm in the middle of the River Walk with Adrian.

With my car dead and living too deep in the country to safely walk the distance even down the long driveway in a dress that hits mid-thigh, I text Adrian to pick me up. Thank God Mom dragged Dad to Home Depot—it'll make it so much easier to fib about my whereabouts later.

When I step out onto the porch, Adrian rounds the bed of the Tacoma, his face lighting up with a thousand-watt beam I've only seen on him once before: when we signed our first record label contract.

Adrian whistles. "Damn, baby," he says, giving me a once over. Make that three times over. "Wouldn't mind bringin' you home tonight."

I slap his shoulder playfully. "You'd bring me home every night if you could."

He catches my hand and brings it to his lips, kissing my fingers with a lopsided smirk.

His dark hair is combed and he's wearing a crisp, dark green button-down with the top three buttons undone, black shorts that hit mid-knee, and fresh Vans. His nose ring glints in the sun that doesn't want to set any time soon.

My gaze lingers on his torso, where his shirt clings in all the right places and show off the tattoos on his neck and chest in a way that'll surely turn heads.

"Damn right, I would." He turns my hand over to kiss my palm, staring straight at me. "Maybe one day you'll let me."

I don't like how that scrambles my thoughts and forces breath to vacate my lungs.

I have to shake myself out of it and pull my hand away. "Where're you takin' me?"

He opens the passenger door of the Tacoma. "You'll see."

I shouldn't be feeling thousands of tiny little blips of excitement in my stomach, and I shouldn't be sidelong glancing over at Adrian driving us into the city, wishing I could have a peek beneath his clothes.

I already know what's under them. We're supposed to be out on a proper *date*, for fuck's sake, not… fucking, for once.

"I'm hoping that smile is because of me, but that might be giving myself too much credit."

I snort. "Your ego is big enough for two."

"Chingonada," he swears, reaching over to pinch my thigh.

Laughing, I try to push his hand away, but he grabs mine. I don't fight him on it. A moment later, he gently squeezes.

Dead brush passes by in the window in a blur. Adrian rubs his thumb across my fingers, and it's only then I realize: we're holding hands. And… it's nice.

When I glance over at him, his simper is breathtaking. It falls when I catch a glimpse of the gauze my dress sleeve mostly hides.

"So," I begin, "Kris is la lechuza. Zak got bit by a vampire baby and made a deal with the devil. You got any legendary qualities you're hiding from me?"

"Yeah. I'm the werewolf of Converse."

I make a face. "Do what now?"

"You've never heard that story?"

"Uh, no. Never. Sounds almost as stupid as fang baby."

"Yeah, fang baby is pretty stupid," he mutters. "I don't think I buy that one, but Kris is pretty real."

I blow air through my teeth. "Yeah, seeing her on the porch last night was scary enough."

My eyes widen like I'm stuck on tracks and a train is headed right for me.

"She's not gonna stop until she gets me. And… and the fucking *devil* has gotta be real, right? Because that's how brujas become lechuzas—"

"Don't worry about Kris. Zak and I will handle her. But you've got to stop going by the bridge, Steph. It's dangerous."

"Yeah, you're telling me!" I squawk.

"Tell you what." He laces our fingers together and brings the back of my hand to his mouth, planting a kiss and glancing between me and the road jamming up with traffic the closer we get to downtown. "I'll promise nothing will happen to you if you do something for me."

"Oh, yeah? And what would that be?"

"Be my girlfriend."

Groaning, I roll my eyes and snatch my hand away. "You're gonna do that, anyway, because I'm your best friend."

"So? It comes with added benefits."

"Like what? Fucking? Because we're doing that already."

"Don't make me revoke your dick privileges."

I cackle loudly. "Do us both a favor!"

"Steph, I don't understand what your problem is," Adrian says. "We're fucking. We're going out. We already know we like each other and get along, for the most part. What else are you waiting for, Zak's blessing?"

"Tsk, fuck you, asshole."

The River Walk winds its way through downtown San Antonio in the windows, greeting us with fiesta-colored lights and flags yelling "Fiesta aqui!" But, fuck, if I'm not in a festive mood at all with Adrian still pestering me about being his girlfriend.

My heart skips a beat and starts to race when Adrian parks in a lot.

The tiniest smile is noticeable on his lips, and it widens when he catches me staring. "What?"

"Promise you won't bother me about being your girlfriend again," I say. "At least let's get through this damn date first like you said."

He stares at me long and hard until, finally, he nods. "Okay. Fair enough." Then, he points at me. "But promise you'll give me a fair shot, hard ass."

I roll my eyes and push the door open. "Fine."

Adrian meets me on the passenger side, where I linger by the door. He watches me curiously, and I have to swallow the unsureness choking me when his honey-brown eyes threaten to remind me of his brother.

"Would going ahead and fucking relieve some of this tension?"

I bark out a laugh. "Excuse me? That's not a real date, sir."

"You're right, but, fuck—this shit is tense, even for a first date."

"You think maybe it's your nerves?" I smart.

"They don't help, but neither do you."

I jab my thumb over my shoulder and start to step away. "I'm totally cool with heading out and pretending like this never happened, then."

Adrian grabs my hand and pulls me close. A light scent of

woody musk shoots straight up my nose and, fuck me, if it doesn't make my mouth water.

His gaze is hypnotic.

"Chill. I don't think either of us want that." He smirks, brushing a lock of hair away from my forehead. "Not tonight."

The thought of smacking that stupid smirk off his face sends a throb pulsing through my core.

My hands ball up into fists.

Adrian glances down, notes the fists, and his smirk becomes more pronounced.

The truck's back door suddenly swings open, and he pushes me. "Get in."

I shove him back. "The hell for?"

But he pushes harder, lifting me up by the ass and making me scoot in all the way as he sits next to me and shuts the door behind him. Drumsticks clatter on the floorboard underfoot.

"What are you doing?"

His hands hook under my knees and tug. "Relieving some of this tension."

CHAPTER 24

DILE

–DON OMAR

ADRIAN YANKS MY LEGS SO HARD THAT I SLIP AND almost hit my head against the door of his truck.

"Oops! Sorry."

His quick grimace makes us both chuckle as he pushes my dress up. Slowly, deliberately, he slips my panties down my legs, maintaining eye contact the whole time as his palms warm my thighs. His lips press against the outside of my calf before practically ripping my underwear off.

His brows quirk with a devilish simper I definitely don't miss as he maneuvers his head between my legs.

Adrian wastes no time, diving in tongue first and not giving me a chance to protest.

I gasp at the wet heat suddenly caressing my clit, moaning airily as I grip onto the seats for dear life. "You do this on every first date?"

"Hell no," he mumbles. His dark eyes meet mine, glittering in the setting sun. He twists his head to kiss my inner thigh. "You're the exception."

He flattens his tongue, licking all the way up my opening

before concentrating on the center of my pleasure. He twirls and swirls all over, making me tremble in one minute flat.

I don't want to enjoy Adrian eating me out in public. I don't want his eyes to lock onto mine, watching me squirm from the pleasure he gives before we even go out on our first date.

I don't even want to be on this stupid date because I know exactly how things will end tonight.

But here I am, moaning for Adrian as his tongue creates an orgasm that grips my core, demanding submission to him and whatever he has up his sleeve for tonight.

He licks me like a dripping popsicle one final time, watching me gulp for breath.

"Convinced yet?"

I lurch forward to smack him over the head.

He yelps out a laugh. "Hey, be nice!"

Scowling at him as I get myself resituated, I reply, "Shut the hell up. You mind handing me my panties?"

"I do mind, actually," he says simply. "Leave 'em off."

I roll my eyes, but I find him staring at me. "What?"

He glances away, shaking his head, before the smirk returns. "You ready to get this date started?"

Groaning, I look over my shoulder into an ever-bustling downtown. It's hot out, and Adrian just made things even worse.

"I need a drink." I nudge his knee. "Go on, git."

He lurches forward, grabbing a napkin off the console and quickly swiping it over his mouth and chin before tossing it to the floorboard. Then, opens the door and holds my hand to help me down.

I try to drop it, but Adrian has a firm grip as he leads me down the street.

"Where are we going, anyway?"

Adrian stops and turns to look up. "Here."

I follow his line of sight "Are you fucking kidding me?"

The grin that cracks his face is way brighter than the Applebee's sign above us. "Yeah, I'm kiddin'."

Leading me a few businesses down, Adrian opens the door to a swanky club and gestures for me to enter.

I wrinkle my nose at him. "Look at you, bein' all cute."

"You're cuter."

"Shut up, I know."

Inside, it's almost pitch black with arctic air blasting over my skin. I reach for Adrian's hand, holding on tightly until my eyes adjust.

He leads me to the backlit bar with liquor bottles lining wooden shelves. When I lean onto the bar, Adrian's body heat warms from my ass to my shoulder blades and over my arms. He gives my bare shoulder a quick kiss before motioning for the bartender and rattling off his order of rum and Coke.

Adrian slips his arms around my waist after I ask for a margarita on the rocks.

His lips come to my ear. "You wanna get hammered and get a hotel room?"

I whack his hand. "Behave!"

"Just sayin' it's an option."

He tries dazzling me with a simper, moving closer. I bump my shoulder into him and turn forward with a beam plastered to my face.

The music bumping through the speakers transitions from house to a familiar but electronic beat, making everyone hoot and holler and rush to the dance floor if they weren't there already.

A deep, throaty chuckle pools in my ear as hands slip to my hips and the body behind me begins to sway, guiding me to the *boom, ba-boom, ba, boom* of reggaeton.

My eyes close and lips curl upward—I haven't heard reggaeton or danced cumbia in a while.

With cold drinks in hand, Adrian doesn't lead me to the dance floor despite two-stepping the way forward. He lugs me along to the other side, just behind a length of tall table separating the dance floor from a section lined with booths and an empty wall leading to restrooms in the back.

I take a long, freezing cold glug of margarita that shocks the heat in my body and sends a shiver down my torso.

Adrian's eyes don't leave me as he gently undulates to the music, his hot hand wrapped around mine while he sips his rum and Coke. His gaze devours me like a predator summing up its prey before striking and, God, I don't want him to stop staring.

I'm suddenly hyper-aware of the fact he didn't give me my panties back.

He sets his drink on the tabletop, taking the liberty of doing the same with mine, and pulls me close. His scent engulfs my senses beyond the smell of alcohol and fog machines and sweat.

He twirls me around before snapping me back to his body. One hand grips mine and the other slinks to the small of my back.

My anatomy responds to his, following his lead in a languid four-step so our bodies stay connected, like we were designed perfectly for each other for this exact moment.

A fever stirs so deeply within that it threatens to consume me.

"What've you been doing since I've been gone, Dree?"

"Besides touring?"

I nod.

"Wondering if you would ever be in my life again."

The music morphs back into regular EDM, cueing us to part and grab our drinks.

I don't respond until I sip more margarita. "Besides the sappy bullshit."

"Getting high and lost in groupie pussy."

My expression sours. "You could've given me the edited version."

"I don't think I'm known for my self-censorship, princesa." He pauses to take a nip. "What about you? The uncensored version."

I hold his gaze, even as it becomes unbearably uncomfortable. "Keeping myself busy at the studio."

He scoffs. "Think you're forgetting something."

"What?"

One of his brows raises sky high. "I know for a fact you went out with Ty at least once while you were there."

I make a face at him. "What's it to you? I've known him way longer than you."

"I wanna know about it."

"It's none of your fucking business."

"Oh, my bad. I thought we were being honest with each other."

"Okay, fine. Ty took me out." I quickly add to get beneath his skin, "*And it was fun.*"

I don't hear it above the music and the din of the crowd surrounding us, but I see him snort. "Yeah, so much fun you came crawling back home and into my bed."

This fucking asshole. "I didn't come back for you."

He looks me up and down, unimpressed. "Coulda fooled me."

"Dree," I snap, turning to fully face him, "what the hell do you want from me? I'm back home. I'm here on a date with you and giving this stupid shit a try like you wanted. What else do you want from me?"

He grabs my hip, fingertips digging in so deeply that nails cut into my skin as he pulls me closer. He cranes down, his nose grazing mine. Embers smolder in his dark eyes. "I am all but on my knees for you."

People dance and talk and holler all around, but it's a whole other world apart from us. His touch and gaze sends an electrical charge flushed with heat down to my core, and my breath catches.

He could be mine.

"Why now?" I demand. Strobe lights pass over his face, highlighting the desperation written all over his face for a split second. "Why not any time before?"

"You were with my brother. You were happy and taken care of—that's all that mattered."

I gnaw on my lip for a moment. "Then why'd you take advantage of the bonfire?"

"Why did you?"

My eyes roll. "I was too drunk and too high to be making any decisions."

"And you think I wasn't?" he retorts. "Steph, what happened that night wasn't right, but, goddamn it, it wasn't a mistake. Not between us, it wasn't."

Drugs and alcohol loosen inhibitions, I remind myself as we stare each other down. It did back then. It did the other night.

Hell, it could again tonight.

I slide my empty drink across the table toward him. "Mind getting us another round?"

He hesitates, but he grabs the condensation-covered glasses and disappears.

I'm left wondering how much of that spiel I buy as I watch him head to the bar. I'm not sure if either of us are deluding ourselves, or if there is a lick of sense in what Adrian is trying to convince me.

Maybe I'll never make heads or tails out of it. It wasn't like I intentionally got so obliterated that night to have an excuse to get away with fucking him—it tore me up so bad afterward that I quit the band and ducked out of town. But I didn't want to break up with Zak, either, not even when we were screaming at each other when I left.

You can't have them both, I tell myself as Adrian finds his way back.

He holds our drinks up high to avoid spilling them, but a woman stops him. His face lights up as she talks, and he nods. Then, she whips out her phone and has a friend take her picture with Adrian before forcing a hug on him.

It's kind of funny when he smiles at them uncomfortably, giving them a nod before rushing back to me.

"What happened to getting lost in groupie pussy?" I smart.

"Ain't the same when the one you really want comes back."

I choose not to say anything else, sipping on a deliciously cold and strong margarita, instead.

"Something never added up for me," Adrian says. He focuses on the dance floor, bodies moving and gyrating to the music. "Yeah, Zak proposing and you telling him no on stage at NYB was embarrassing, and having to work together afterwards woulda been pretty damn hard, but not impossible. Nothing to fuckin' leave town over." His throat bobs, and his eyes avert to the table. "Was there something else?"

My mouth runs dry, so dry that not even chugging a whole margarita helps. Peering up, he finally meets my gaze.

"Was there something else?" he repeats firmly.

I hesitate. Just even mentioning how much worse it could have been makes the reality force its way back into the present when I had long buried it under devotion to work.

"I… I thought so. But the day I moved into my apartment in Atlanta, I finally got my period."

Adrian exhales so sharply that I reach out to grab and

hold him close, just in case he goes tumbling backwards. I swear, I could see stars swirling in his eyes.

It takes a long, strobe- and bass-filled moment before Adrian slips an arm across my back, gripping me to him so tightly. His voice is gruff in my ear. "You should've told me. You should've fucking *stayed*."

"It's nothing that concerned you—"

"Are you out of your fucking mind?" he says loudly. Heads turn in my periphery. "You think I would've wanted you to go through that alone?"

My brows furrow as I gape at him. "It's my choice."

"And I would've supported you." He searches my face. "No matter what, Steph. I would've been there if you'd just let me."

Scanning the bar and a second empty margarita glass, hugging Adrian to reassure him that things are okay, I have to remind myself we're supposed to be on a real first date and not hashing out our pre-existing relationship woes. It's hard, though, when the guy just won't let up.

Adrian takes a long pull from his drink. After he sets the glass down, his hands travel to my hips to make them swing with his. My arms come up around his shoulders, hands resting behind his neck, letting him direct my body with his.

A "Despacito" remix thrums through the atmosphere, making me groan and complain if it's still popular. Adrian assures me it still is.

"Tell me something, Dree," I start. "What is it you actually like about me? Not no superficial bullshit, either."

If there's a way to permanently smack the smirk off his face, I want to know about it.

His hands aren't overly suggestive, for once. "I like that you're a ride-or-die kind of person. That you're smart and fuckin' fierce and go for what you want. That you're an incredible musician and always trying to improve. I love that you love being a tia and went above and beyond for la prince-sita when Kris couldn't be here." His gaze flares. "That you love me and my brother to a fault."

"I never said that I love you," I insist. "Not like that."

He bends to my ear. "You don't have to."

His lips graze the corner of my mouth. The contact jolts my flesh and I yank myself away, escaping to a blank space of wall to just *breathe*.

I watch him a few feet away sipping on his rum and Coke while keeping a careful eye on me. When I'm assured he's staying put, I take a deep breath and close my eyes.

The wall is cool and smooth on my back; a sad attempt at cooling the fire burning beneath my skin. Tequila and lime and salt coat my tongue, and it makes me want to keep drinking the night away, maybe until I let Adrian whisk me away to a hotel room to spend another night together in total bliss inside our own bubble.

My arm hurts a little when my skin prickles from cold air blowing directly on me.

He could be mine.

When I open my eyes, Adrian is still in the same spot surveying the dance floor. Colorful lights revolve over the floor and shine on something that makes me double take to make sure I'm not seeing a snake or some shit in a fucking club, even though that wouldn't surprise me—we've had snakes get into the house a time or two before.

I follow the lights, lingering on a chicken foot and a hoof.

My brows knit together and follow the taloned claw and glistening hoof up legs attached to Adrian sipping on his drink.

CHAPTER 25

NOTHING'S OVER

–Day/Four

BREATHING IN SHARPLY, I SHAKE MY HEAD AND blink a few times. God, I hope there's nothing extra in my fucking margaritas because I *cannot* handle Adrian having a chicken foot and a hoof for feet right now.

Just what I need: for my date to be San Antonio's dancing devil.

Refocusing, Adrian's feet are normal and he's still wearing his Vans.

He catches me staring and sets his drink down before sauntering over.

The warmth of his body heats my front as he posts his arm above my shoulder on the wall, drawing closer.

I hesitate, looking away and making his mouth land on the hollow of my ear. But that doesn't stop him from kissing up and down my neck.

Peeking down, his feet are normal.

Adrian captures my chin and forces me to look at him. He searches my eyes, slowly moving closer, until he kisses me softly.

All sorts of colors flicker beyond my eyelids as the

thumping of bass pulses through the atmosphere. Adrian's hand warms my neck, and his thumb pressing down on my chin coaxes my lips apart.

His mouth is cold and sweet with the smallest burn and a hint of sex. The woody musk he's wearing forces all thoughts out of my head and allows only memories of his touch to consume my brain.

The nightclub doesn't exist outside of us—we're not surrounded by bodies bumping along with the music echoing through the darkness. It's just me and Dree, only us in the swirling lights and house music with lips locked and eyes closed.

My arms slip around his shoulders to draw him closer, pressing all of myself against him. His hands slip down to grab handfuls of ass, and he grinds us into each other.

"For Christ's sake, Dree, what is your problem?"

We pull apart immediately at the sound of a familiar voice.

Brandy stands next to us with a couple of drinks in hand.

Her eyes and nostrils both flare on me. "So it's true. What the fuck is wrong with y'all?"

Adrian straightens and grabs my hand, but I pipe up before he has the chance. "I didn't know he was seeing someone."

"Bullshit," she spits. "And this is what you left town over—"

Adrian says loudly, "It's not her fault, so back off."

Her blazing glower sets in on me. "What the fuck, Steph?"

Grimacing, I don't know what to tell her except, "Please don't say anything to anyone."

With cold glasses in hand, she fans out fingers around them like she's surrendering. "Don't worry—I won't even say anything to you," she says before stalking off.

If I thought Brandy was going to be the hardest sell before, I just lost her for good.

Adrian squeezes my hand. "Hey, don't worry about her. She'll come around."

My nose scrunches, and I turn away as I cross my arms. "I don't think so."

He catches me and makes me look at him. "I think if you stop ghosting and start reaching out, she'd be more amenable."

I bite the inside of my lip and stare at the dark floor shimmering from spilled drinks. "This was a mistake."

Adrian reaches for me, but I slip away, slinking through bodies between me and the door.

It's hard to breathe in a hundred-and-one degree weather that tries to suffocate anyone trying to live their fucking life out here.

Adrian catches me before I reach the crosswalk, blocking my way. "Steph, wait."

I skirt past. "We shouldn't be doing this."

He grabs my hand and drags me toward the parking lot. "We've done worse."

Scoffing, I try to snatch my hand back, but he has a firm grip. "Seriously? That's supposed to make me feel better?"

He stops and steadies me by the shoulders when I run into him. "No, it's not."

Pretty sure there's steam coming out of my ears. "Then what the fuck, Dree?"

"It's a reminder that we've done some shitty things that we're trying to make right." He takes my hands, letting them hang between us as he stares down. "All anyone's gonna see is the shitty things you did in a moment of weakness, no matter how much good you do or how much you wanna make things right."

I'm all too familiar with the feeling that weighs down my

limbs; it's kept me company obsessively for the past year and a half and has refused to let me shake it off.

As I search Adrian's features, understanding starts to push it aside.

He's just been shitty because of me. And I've been shitty because of him.

Maybe he's right: maybe we're awful people because we've been delaying the inevitable between us.

I've been denying it.

I squeeze Adrian's hand, pulling him out of deep thought and back to the sidewalk with me. "You know what I like about you?"

The corner of his mouth pinches. "What?"

"I like that you're relentless and bullheaded. That you're such a badass at what you do and you know it. That beneath your snarky asshole exterior you're actually a really sweet goofball and care so deeply about so much."

I pause, eyeballing the small white scar just below his hairline from an accident when we were on tour for our second album. He got too drunk when we were in Canada and fell down some stairs. A small smile tugs at my lips, remembering the way he cackled his ass off at my terror watching blood pour down his face.

"I like that you still see the best in me even if I think I've lost it."

Adrian's hands cup my cheeks and stroke my hair away from my face. He leans down, but I turn away.

My brows furrow and I bite down on my lip, avoiding his gaze. "I'm still not sure about this."

"Guess you better figure it out quick."

I huff, but don't respond. His ex basically blasted me on social media, now Brandy caught us—he's right.

Adrian studies me silently for a moment before pulling

me close to kiss my forehead. In the Tacoma, he reaches for my hand as soon as he maneuvers onto the busy road.

The quiet in the truck is uncomfortable. When I finally peek over at him, his features are pulled down as he glares at the road.

The gash on my arm pulsates. I groan softly and scowl.

He glimpses at my arm where the gauze peeks out. "You okay?"

I nod. "Just stings a little."

He gives my hand a small, reassuring squeeze, but all I can see each time I blink is the chicken foot and hoof on the dance floor.

"Sorry tonight was a bit of a bust," Adrian pipes up. "I'll think of something better for next time."

I scoff. "Who said there's gonna be a next time?"

"Me," he says with a wistful smile.

Rolling my eyes, I tell him, "You know, plenty of first dates end disastrously. Surprised this one didn't get any worse."

"Tsk, really? Why you gotta be so fuckin' mean."

"Why do you have to be such an asshole all the time?"

"So I've been an asshole all night, huh?"

I grumble under my breath and stare out the passenger window, watching dimly-lit mesquite and huisache and live oaks pass by in a blur. My fingers tap in an erratic pattern with no sense of rhythm, wondering why he's still holding my hand.

"Dree?"

"Hm?"

"For trying so hard for us to be a thing, we sure do fight a lot."

"Psh, so?"

"Don't you ever get tired of fighting and arguing with the girl you love?"

"No," he immediately answers. "Just means that we care so much. Plus, the makeup sex will be incredible."

I snort before a long pause consumes the cab. "Since when?"

"What?"

"You've loved me since when?"

He doesn't answer right away with a smart-ass remark. Glimpsing over, his anger has evaporated, replaced by awe.

His thumb rubs back and forth across the backs of my fingers, I think more out of nervousness instead of affection. "Do you really wanna know?"

I give a small nod.

It takes a long, torturous moment before he answers. "Steph, I've loved you ever since Robbie introduced us after church." He chuckles softly. "Never thought I'd willingly sit through religious ed and Mass just to stare at my best friend's sister for an hour and a half once a week."

My brows knit together. "And you never said anything?"

He doesn't respond.

I guess we're a *lot* more alike than I want to think. Cowardice and all.

He remembers the exact moment he fell in love with me over fifteen years later. I was in third grade and I wasn't thinking about boys yet—I was busy figuring out how to mangle my fingers into chords on the Epiphone Dad gave me for my birthday that year. Long before Zak and I were even a thought.

But it doesn't change anything.

I still shared life with Zak for six years. I still regret screwing everything up.

I still love Zak, and a part of me always will.

Adrian pulls up to the house, circling the pecan tree to face the driveway and park. The porch light is on; colors flash over curtains in the window, so Mom and Dad are home watching TV in the living room.

Adrian sighs and runs his hand through his hair, pushing his head against the headrest and looking down his nose at the drive. "Zak asked you out before I got the cajones to do it. I... I got so fucking tongue tied every time I tried. Zak mighta asked you first, but, in some weird way, it meant you were mine, too."

He finally meets my gaze. "We've fucked up a lot because of each other. This whole thing is messed up because I slept with my brother's girlfriend, and it's so much worse 'cause I still want her even though y'all aren't over each other. I just... I finally got a taste of what it would be like to keep you, and I'm not about to let that go."

CHAPTER 26

THESE WALLS

–DREAM THEATER

THE HURRICANE CHURNING INSIDE SEIZES THE breath in my lungs. This diabolical creation of two men that have staked their claim in my life has hurled me through so many dark and lonely nights, left me wondering if I did the right thing refusing Zak's proposal and leaving him and his brother both behind only with the words "I quit."

Part of me swoons over Adrian's confession.

The rest of me is left wondering if he meant it as an underhanded threat.

But the longer I stare at him, the more I understand it's a vow—a sweet and romantic, fucked up, dangerous vow.

"Steph, I don't know what you actually think about me—"

"I spent six years dating Zak. I planned a life with your brother, and I had to go fuck it all up with you. What are you hoping for if we're together? What do you see in the future for us?"

Adrian shifts in his seat. The leather creaks. "All I see is you and me, princesa. The future is beyond me."

"Don't you think that's part of the problem? I want to get married one day. I want to have a family. I want to grow old with someone, to watch our kids grow up and have them help out at the festival just like I did. My family has a legacy beyond Timeless I want to pass down to mine and Robbie's kids, but I want to be with someone who wants to be active in all of it. I want someone who can see and plan for that kind of future with me."

He rubs his chin, staring out the windshield with an indiscernible expression illuminated by dashboard lights.

"I know you don't want any of that, Dree," I say. "What we have is just... it's just a good time, I guess. But it's nothing more than that. It can't be."

He sighs heavily, pursing his lips at the waxing moon hanging in the sky. "You ever think I said I didn't want those things because you're the only girl I wanted all that with? Because... what's the point in doing any of it when your girl got away? The white wedding, the white picket fence, the kids—what does any of it matter when your one and only is with your twin?"

We don't dare look at one another, letting the dark silence in the cab consume us.

I thought tonight was supposed to be fun.

"Would you change anything about that night?" I ask. "After all this, would you have smoked or drank less, or slept in the front seat, something?"

Adrian shakes his head vehemently. "Don't fucking play that game, Steph. We can't change what happened."

"Just answer me."

"No," he says firmly. "If you're asking if I wish I didn't betray my brother, then, yeah, I do wish that. I wish I'd've had the fuckin' balls to tell you how I felt before he asked you out. He said he forgives me, but I don't forgive myself for it."

My bottom lip trembles. "He said he doesn't forgive me."

"For leaving," Adrian clarifies. "Zak is gonna love you forever. But you leaving for Atlanta fucking destroyed him."

"Then why take me out on a date, huh?" I yell, turning in my seat to face him. "If you know Zak is always gonna feel that way, and you don't forgive yourself for what we did, why are you trying so goddamn hard to be with me?"

Adrian grabs my jaw. His nostrils flare with each heavy exhale. "Because you're mine just as much as you are his. You get that, princesa? You might've been Zak's first, but you've always been mine. You've always been *ours*."

My face suddenly smashes into his, lips pressing hard against his as my fingers tangle in his hair to pull him closer.

"C'mere," he growls against my mouth.

Somehow, I swing myself over the console and straddle him. He takes my chin and leads my mouth to his, the desperation in the trembling of his lips and hands on me blasting desire straight through my core.

I bunch my dress out of the way and reach for the steering wheel behind me to raise myself up from his lap. He quickly unbuttons and pulls his shorts down.

His erect cock slapping my pussy makes me gasp softly. Adrian guides his dick along the slickness waiting for him, priming us both before he positions himself at my entrance.

Gently, he spreads me apart with his girth. When I sink down, we groan simultaneously.

Stars swirl and twinkle between us.

He yanks the neckline of my dress so hard that fabric quietly rips. Cool air from the AC flows over my bare chest and my nipples pebble. His arms wrap around me, and he peppers kisses over my chest, up and down my neck.

I cling to his shoulders as I ride.

"Why do you feel so good," I whine in his ear.

His hands still my face, making me stare at him. "Because you're a fucking Ramos slut."

I whimper loudly as my eyes close, hips swaying over his.

He forces me further down to take all of him, every last inch until I'm full and completely wrapped around him.

His moan is a goosebump-inducing melody. "You've always taken me so well."

"Better than any groupie?"

"Better than anyone," he rasps, his hips bumping up into mine.

"Why do you want me so bad?" I whisper.

His lips lock onto mine for the longest moment. We both moan and groan at the slightest movement of my hips, from Adrian's cock swelling against the tightness of my inner walls.

With his hand caressing my cheek, I gaze into his piercing stare through the darkness. "I love you."

Maybe I've always known.

The way he would look at me during class or practice. The way his eyes light up when I walk into a room. How he sends a message every day even if he knows I'll ignore it. How he goes out of his way to get under my skin.

Maybe a part of me has always known that Adrian Ramos loves me like his twin brother does.

I force a hand between us to press fingers against my clit, desperately bouncing up and down on him and clenching my core so tightly that he whines.

I'm so close, and I want Adrian to come in me.

I want to be his, too.

"Right there, baby," he murmurs.

My fingers move in harsh circles over my clit.

"Fuck."

The moan that escapes me is shrill and loud. "Dree..."

He captures a nipple in his mouth, sucking and making me gyrate harder, faster. I don't care anymore if movement in the truck is noticeable from the outside.

"Dree," I repeat breathily, on the precipice of losing it.

He whimpers into my chest, his moans soaring higher until he slams all the way into me.

The world shatters into a colorful kaleidoscope that paints everything in brilliant crimson and indigo and gold. It leaves everything with a peculiar new shimmer and sparkle that wasn't there before, a dazzle that leaves me fumbling, blindly bumbling my way through foreign territory.

I like it here.

And it's fucking terrifying.

I'm left clinging to Adrian, gasping for breath in his ear and pulsating around his cock as orgasm flows through me, as his come fills me to the brim. "Oh, my God."

His breathing is ragged as I kiss the hollow of his ear. The vein in his neck pulses under my lips as I trail down his throat. He captures my chin and presses his mouth to mine.

Adrian kisses me as if I hold all the precious oxygen left in this world and he's on his final breath.

Or maybe like he finally made love to the girl he adores instead of hate-fucking her.

"Goddamn it, I wanna take you home with me."

I don't want to tell him no.

Instead, I kiss him again, wishing I could go home with him without upsetting anyone. I want to cuddle up to Adrian after making love, to let him whisper sweet nothings until we both drift to sleep in each other's arms.

But I want the same with Zak, too.

I want him to hold me tight, to kiss me until I'm breathless and starving for him, to murmur how much he still loves me and wants me to be here.

But they're brothers. *Twin brothers.*

I was with Zak for so long, I fucked everything up so badly with him and the Ramos family that I can't have either of them the way I want.

After resituating my neckline, I reach for the steering

wheel to lift myself up, and we both groan as his dick slips out. His come seeps down my thighs as I fall into the passenger seat.

Adrian reaches for my hand and laces our fingers together. He kisses the back of my hand. "Steph..."

He doesn't say anything else, only peers over at me.

The gash on my arm suddenly burns and stings, making me inhale sharply and grab my arm. "Fuck. When's this shit supposed to stop hurting."

Adrian doesn't respond. When I look up, I find him focused ahead at the line of trees.

A gigantic white owl with long black hair perches in a live oak strong enough to handle a human-sized bird on its limbs.

Kris's face with an ivory beak flushed crimson and black eyes stares back at us a short distance away.

Correction: she stares at *me*, her tongue flitting out to wet her bloody beak like she's extra hungry and waiting for me to step foot outside the truck.

Chapter 27

The House (That Fear Built)

–Toothgrinder

I NEVER THOUGHT I WOULD BE THE STUFF OF legends, being one of the unfortunate souls to incur the wrath of a man-eating, shapeshifting witch literally hunting me down until she's got my beating heart in her beak.

I never thought she would be someone so close, either.

Adrian cracks his door open. "Wait here."

He's sure to fully close the door, examining his owl-sister by the truck for a moment. Suddenly, he throws his arms up in the air and flails around, yelling curse words at her.

She beats her wings at him a couple of times, obviously irritated with him getting in the way of her dinner.

Adrian doesn't give a shit; he smacks her wings, unafraid of la lechuza, and yells, "No me chingues, go! Pinche pendeja!"

Kris gets the last word whacking him over the head with her wing before soaring off, heading west.

Normally, that'd be pretty funny. If anything about la lechuza was funny, I mean.

He stands watch with fists on his hips until she disappears into the horizon over the trees. He remains at attention for a long moment, probably waiting, watching, listening for Kris to fly back around and grab me when we least expect it.

She seems to have left, though, so he returns to the truck, opening my door and holding his hand out for me to grab and hop down. The second my feet hit the pavement, his hand is on my cheek and his lips on mine.

A door squeaks open. "Stephani?"

"Shit," I whisper. Slowly, I turn around to find Mom watching us from the porch with her arms crossed over her bright blue muumuu and a brow raised. "Ma'am?"

"What was all that racket?"

"Oh, you know," Adrian interjects, "just scaring off la lechuza."

Mom rolls her eyes. "Y'all've been sitting out here for fifteen minutes," she comments. "Better not be doin' anything inappropriate."

He leans against the Tacoma in earnest like I didn't just ride his dick and his come isn't seeping down my thighs. "No, ma'am," Adrian lies through his teeth.

Mom isn't amused. "You and Robbie both have always been my problem children."

Adrian gasps, slapping his hand over his heart. "I'm offended! We both know I'm the golden child."

Mom scoffs. "Mmm-hm." Her glare sets in on me. "C'mon before I drag you to confession tomorrow."

Adrian grabs my hip and bends to my ear, saying lowly, "Don't tell her you're gonna need to go every day this week to repent for what we've done and are gonna do."

I spin around and smack his shoulder. "Shut the hell up, damn fool."

He grins impishly before waving at Mom. "Make sure our girl behaves. Father Tomas is relentless in the confessional."

Mom clucks her tongue and bitches at him under her

breath. When I step onto the porch, I catch some semblance of "pain in the ass" before stepping into the house.

I start heading to my room until Mom calls out, "What are you doing?"

Looking over my shoulder at her with brows knitted, I reply, "Going to my room?"

Her arms are still firmly crossed as she steps closer to me with a terrifyingly serious expression. "I meant with Adrian."

I turn around to face her and shrug. "We went out, had a couple of drinks. Stuff people in their twenties normally do."

Mom's knowing stare is one of those that makes you squirm and could make you confess to anything just to get her to stop.

She sucks on her teeth. "Are you and Adrian dating?"

I shift from foot to foot, hesitating. "What if we are?"

"I don't think it's a good idea."

"Why?"

"Because God forbid you rejoin Timeless, make another mistake, and think leaving town is the only way out of things again."

The scowl on my face sinks lower into a sullen, brooding frown. "I'm not getting back in the band."

"You really should."

Scoffing, I spin around and stalk off toward the house.

"Listen to the last album, if you haven't," Mom hollers after me down the hall. "It's pretty great."

All I can respectfully muster is a loud Frankenstein grunt to acknowledge I heard and to not come banging on my door about it.

I push my back against the cool door, holding my breath and listening for footsteps.

Mom heads back to the living room. The TV shuts off. Their bedroom door closes on the other side of the house.

I finally take a deep breath and let my eyes close.

My phone buzzes. Dree texted a kissy face and heart emojis.

Even though I went into the shower all lightheaded with a big grin plastered to my face, I'm left staring up at the dark ceiling in bed solemnly with a familiar emptiness in the pit of my stomach.

A part of me wishes I would've let Adrian whisk me away back to his bed.

But Zak is probably there at the other end of the house.

With him nearby, he might be all that I think about even while Adrian is inside me.

Huffing, I reach for my phone and pull up something I've already searched for recently: *Zak Ramos, Timeless.*

The same photo pops up of Zak riling up a crowd at a concert, the one that goes with the article about the song he wrote.

The song he wrote to get over me, on the album I've never heard.

Just as quickly as the thought entered my mind, I jump up from bed to search through my suitcase for earbuds, plugging them in and queuing it up to play from my phone.

The intro song starts off strong with a driving, heavily distorted guitar riff that sends blood pulsing through my veins at an alarming rate.

Zak has always sent my heart into overdrive—in the studio, on stage, and in life.

Bass kicks in, complicated and heavy and low, something that my brother has probably been sitting on for ages, aching to use a heavily prog-inspired riff.

Cymbals crash, a snare snaps, and toms and double kicks thrum, pulsating in my eardrums and making my breath catch.

The music cuts out suddenly.

Shannon's voice starts as a menacing whisper.

If you could see me now
you'd never know what's coming.

He repeats it again and again and again, until there's a measure of rest.

A low growl rumbles, and the album starts with an even bigger bang than I thought possible.

They. Were. *Pissed.*

And it's so much harder than the three albums we wrote before.

Timeless blasts into my ears as I search through cardboard boxes I arrived home with just two days ago, frantically searching for the packages Shannon sent. A few songs play before I find them stuffed at the bottom of a box I knew I wouldn't bother opening for quite some time.

I stare at the unopened things on my bed for a whole song like they're Pandora's Box and, if opened, could possibly bring the downfall and destruction of anything and everything I hold dear.

Guess it's good those things are few and far between these days.

Opening the box with the oldest post date, all sorts of things tumble out: an album signed by all the guys in silver Sharpie, a couple of shirts, a lanyard, a postcard. The card is from Shannon, writing that he hoped working at the studio was fun and that him and Andrea and everyone missed me.

Seeing her crayon scribble fills my eyes with tears.

I hold up the first shirt. TIMELESS stamped across the chest in white text over a black shirt with a refreshed shattered clock logo beneath it is a sight to behold.

The second shirt unfurls and a white envelope falls onto the bed below. I reach for the envelope and take a peek at the little bit of black scrawled over the front.

My name in Zak's handwriting.

Whatever's in here, I'm extra careful with it just from

seeing my name in his writing, as if it's a sacred text that could crumble with the smallest wrong movement.

Inside is just a folded piece of notebook paper with more scribbles that I delicately unfold. Zak's handwriting is atrocious, but I can make out the title written out at the very top of the page.

Dawn

The Timeless song flowing between my ears now is different from the rest and every other song we've ever composed.

The low, husky voice ringing in my ears isn't Shannon's.

She could be the devil,
and I'd still give her my soul.

Chapter 28

Intoxicated

–Now And On Earth

My face is hot and puffy and snotty. Tissues dot my bedspread among Timeless merch and pile on the floor. The Timeless shirt on me smells like plastic and musty old cardboard, but I don't care.

Zak sings to me through my earbuds. Sings *about* me, forever immortalized in the most popular Timeless track to date.

He's been on repeat for a couple of hours. I can't bear to let the rest of the album play. Not yet.

"Dawn" isn't as depressing as I thought it would sound. Electronics kick in after the hushed, husky intro, and Zak's clean vocals come back strong and orotund, lacing and flowing with Shannon's gutturals that send the song into a new echelon I never thought possible for Timeless.

She could be the devil
  and I'd still give her my soul
  A midnight prayer so bleak
  God can't fill this hole
  But a new day is coming

this I know to be true
and it starts with my dawn
You never should've gone
This night won't end (it won't fucking end)
I can't get you out of my head
till I can call you mine once again
So take me back
Can we go back to the beginning?
Let it go, let it go
Just let it all go
'Cause I can't stand it here
I need you near
I wish you'd come back
and bring me my dawn
You never should've gone
This night won't end (it won't fucking end)
I can't get you out of my head
till I can call you mine once again
She could be the devil
and I'd still give her my soul
But we just couldn't see
the devil in me.

My bottom lip trembles. I can't stop sniveling.
The lyrics Zak wrote are still clutched to my chest.
My hair is soaked with tears.
I'm out of tissues.
I should call him.
A sob slips when I reach for my phone and realize what I'm doing.
I don't even have his number anymore.
I shouldn't bother—there's no way he feels the same now.
He even said it in that interview: he wrote it to get it out of his system, and he got over it.

He said it the other night: he doesn't forgive me.

But Dree said he doesn't forgive me for leaving.

If Saturday was his last day alive, his one regret would've been not kissing me one last time.

And I keep spitting in his face hooking up with my personal demon, his twin brother.

Finally, I let the rest of the album play.

Timeless has always been fucking amazing. Shannon, Robbie, Zak, and Adrian all are talented beyond measure. This album has incredible depth—the production is unreal.

Timeless might have started off as Dream Theater and Pantera after-school jam sessions between Robbie and the twins, but I'm the one who literally dragged Shannon into the music room and demanded that they have him on vocals and do more than covers.

Timeless didn't become a thing until I agreed to join on guitar—Robbie and the twins refused to budge on becoming a real band until I was with them.

Timeless was *my* fucking band.

But, now, they've staked their own claim without me. Timeless has only gotten better, and so have the guys, no matter how much they bellyache about missing the good ol' days.

They're good and old for a reason.

While I'm supposed to be hard at work on graphics for New Year's Ball, it's ten in the morning and I'm still in bed, wearing my Timeless shirt and listening to "Dawn" on repeat. Still surrounded by piles of used tissues and everything Shannon sent me.

My phone buzzes in my hand.

Good morning princesa. Could I interest you in tacos?

> Morning. Think I'm gonna hit up the coffee pot and get to work.

> You're just now getting up?

> Yeah

> Ok. I love you

I stare at his text for a moment too long, knowing he's waiting for me to text back.

The aching gnaw in my gut keeps Zak front and center of my mind.

There's a song out in the world about me and what I did to him.

Yet his brother has his claws sunk so deep into me that I can't shake it off anymore.

Finally, I send a kissy emoji, hoping that'll satisfy him for now.

Mom cleared off a spot on my bed to sit and has been quietly stroking my hair for what feels like an eternity.

"I don't think I'll make it to work today," I finally whisper.

"Sure you will," she responds a lot more cheerfully than I care for. "Just a late start and early finish." She kisses my head. "I'll get a fresh pot of coffee started for you."

I stay in bed just a little longer, staring up at the ceiling. The scent of coffee permeates my room.

My phone buzzes.

> Band meeting @ 8. It's important. U should be there too, Steph.

My head crashes into a pillow, staring at Shannon's text.

If a Timeless meeting is important enough to warrant me being there, it's definitely nothing good.

Especially if Robbie isn't part of the group text calling for a band meeting.

"Stephani! Coffee!"

When I round the corner of the kitchen, Dad is helping himself to a fresh cup.

"Mornin', sweet pea." He pecks the top of my head as I reach for a mug.

I feel his questioning gaze on me, but he doesn't ask anything.

"So I won't bombard you today," he starts, "but I do wanna go over a quick list of things that need to get done pronto."

I lean back against a counter with a steaming cup of coffee at my lips. "Promo video, social media posts, shirt design mockups, VIP and backstage and press passes…" I trail off, tapping the mug and thinking. "Oh, and posters, duh."

Mom reaches over to smack his shoulder, startling him. "I told you she's on top of everything."

"I'd hope so after all these years," Dad says, watching me with a glint of pride. He blinks and brings coffee to his lips, mentioning under his breath, "Now all that's left is getting you back in the band."

I click my tongue and scoff, taking my coffee with me to his office to get started on promo material and hoping that'll take my mind off everything.

When I sit down at my old workstation in the office, I pause to scroll through socials, just to bullshit a minute longer before getting to work.

But the red dot showing ninety-nine-plus notifications waiting for me has my eyes widening and my back straightening up like a bolt of lightning just struck.

I'm tagged in so many posts featuring photos and videos of my surprise appearance at the show on Saturday night.

Interspersed between those is the occasional notification of a comment tagging me in Norma's post.

> This bitch? @Stephani Wade

> Check out who might be back in Timeless!!! @Stephani Wade

> UMMMMM SURPRISE GUEST APPEARANCE AT THE TIMELESS SHOW BY THEEEE @STEPHANI WADE??!?!?!! *FANGIRLING*

> OMG sum of these hoes just want to set fire to shit when theyre jealous. @Stephani Wade u should b ashamed of urself!

> Please tell me you're coming back to Timeless @Stephani Wade!!!

> Dont tell me @Stephani Wade got BOTH Ramos twins. Thats SO not fair!!

> @Stephani Wade whore

Without giving it a second thought, I deactivate my account for now—I'll deal with the weekend's aftermath when I'm not already feeling like I'm six feet underground.

Another text message pops up, this time in the family chat from my brother.

> Dinner at yalls place Wednesday?

Great, I think, slumping back into my chair. Just what I need: being face to face with my ex-best friend who hates my guts and my brother who is oblivious to tonight's secret band meeting.

What's next, Kris is going to show up unannounced and rip my heart out for the main course?

CHAPTER 29

IREMIA

–So It Begins

Foul is one way to describe my mood as I wring the steering wheel of my car on the way to the twins'. Dad just gave me a stern talking to about keeping up with maintenance on my car, and I had to come up with some new excuse for leaving other than partying.

But how do I explain I'm going to a band meeting that Robbie doesn't know about, but, no, I'm not rejoining the band?

This can't be good, I think as I pull into the driveway and find Shannon stepping out of his dark gray Ford truck. With more rumors spreading like wildfire throughout the day and Robbie being out of the know of tonight's band meeting, something's up.

The way Shannon eyeballs me as I park behind his truck confirms it.

"Hey, you made it," he says far too cheerfully.

"Yeah, about that," I say as I approach with crossed arms. "Why am I here?"

He cocks his head and ambles toward the front door. "How was work?"

"Would've been a lot better if I didn't have this hangin' over my head all day."

"C'mon, Steph," he says as he opens the heavy wooden door without knocking. "It's nothing bad, I promise."

"Yeah, right," I grumble under my breath as I pass him by.

Dree lounges on the leather sectional with his vape, and Zak is perched at the other end frowning at his phone through his glasses. His wavy hair is down for the first time since I've been back, and it's only gotten longer, stopping mid-torso.

I stop in my tracks. A sudden chill works its way down my spine—I haven't been in the same room as both Ramos brothers in a while.

Shannon nudges me forward, catching Dree's attention. He flashes a bright smile at me as Shannon pushes me toward the center of the sectional—between the twins.

Zak doesn't pay any attention to me, staying focused on his phone. No bandage covers up holes in his neck—he's completely healed with no indication of being attacked.

Maybe *I'm* the one who's been drunk and hallucinating the weekend away.

"Hey," Dree greets, pushing himself up on an elbow as Shannon heads into the kitchen. "How was work?"

I shrug. "Fine."

Dree watches me with that lingering smile, even as he vapes. "Okay."

My gaze wanders to the mantle above the fireplace, full with photo frames. Scanning from left to right, none of the photos have changed—it's the same mix of family and travel photos from tours. A couple of them include me smiling brightly and hugging onto Zak, him wearing the signature Ramos smirk that lingers between happy and smug as he squeezes me tight.

I swallow hard and look away when a cloud of vapor

envelops the photos. I highly doubt Dree has mentioned our date to his brother.

Shannon reappears with a bottle of Shiner in hand.

"Okay, important band meeting," I say loudly as he sits in a leather armchair across from me. "Why am I involved?"

"Oh, you're gonna love this."

My jaw clenches. "Oh, am I?"

Zak groans, tosses his phone aside on the couch, and pinches the bridge of his nose beneath the frames on his face. He doesn't look so hot, appearing wan. "Spit it out already, Jesus."

Shannon hardly glances at Zak as he raises his phone in the air. "My inbox has been blowin' up all damn day with labels askin' if you're comin' back to the band and if we've signed another contract yet."

I don't say a peep as I glare at him.

He happily goes on, "Even Tom Vargas emailed me."

"Fuck Tom Vargas," the twins and I simultaneously bitch. Safe to say we all remember Tom's bitch behavior blasting me online when we refused to sign with his sad label back in the day.

Shannon snorts and nods. "Yeah, I told him where he could stick it." He leans forward and rests his elbows on his knees. "I say we pull the fuckin' trigger and do this."

I make a face. "Do what?"

His palms spread, facing the ceiling. "You come back to the band."

Without hesitation, I tell him straight up, "No."

"Tsk, why not?"

"Because it's a bad idea." I rub a hand over my face that's gone without makeup today. "Not sure if you noticed what happened when I was last with the band."

Adrian waves it off. "With as many fights as Rob's started on stage, nobody remembers."

I keep my focus trained on the brown carpet and practically yell, "I'm talking about my ex-goddamn-boyfriend not being cool with it."

Zak throws his hands in the air. "Did I ever fuckin' say I wasn't? Maybe you don't remember me tellin' you I didn't want you to go."

My glare sets in on him. "Fine. But don't talk to me that way."

His eyes close and head falls back. "Don't assume you know what I want."

"Are you okay?" I question. "You don't look so good."

Zak shrugs the question off and settles further into the couch. "Think I finally drank too much."

Rolling my eyes and shaking my head, I let it drop.

"See, Zak's fine with it," Shannon says. "We all want you back."

"So you mind telling me why Robbie's not here, then?"

"He needs to fuckin' go," Adrian spits.

"Yeah, he does," Zak grumbles in agreement.

My head slowly shakes. "I don't know why y'all are suddenly mortal enemies after all these years, but if Timeless isn't the same without me, then it's definitely not the same without Rob."

Shannon waves me off. "I just need to know if you'll come back, Steph."

I stare long and hard at the floor for a moment. "Y'all have done better without me."

Zak sighs audibly. His eyes are still closed, face aimed toward the ceiling with his head resting against the back of the couch. "You know how much better we could've been *with* you?"

Adrian nods in my periphery. "The last album was great, but it wasn't as great as it coulda been if you were still here."

I bite down on my bottom lip, chewing as I pick at my

nails and begin to shake my foot. "Do you think Robbie will calm down if I come back?"

It takes a long moment before Adrian says, "He might. But I've got a feeling he's still gonna stick his nose where it don't belong."

Shannon huffs. "Bet."

I make a face. "The hell does that mean?"

The silence that descends in the room is eerie. Shannon picks at the label on his bottle of beer. Zak keeps his eyes closed and arms crossed. Dree vapes, sending a fresh, thick cloud out into the middle of the room.

"He's blaming y'all for me leaving, right?" I ask, glancing between Z and Dree. My palms spread open and turn toward the ceiling. "I'll come clean and tell him what really happened. He can't be pissed at y'all when I'm the problem."

Adrian swings his legs over the side of the couch and sits upright, his intense focus burning solely on me. "You're not the problem, Steph."

Zak finally uncrosses his arms and sits up, opening his eyes. They look so dark against the paleness of his skin. He grimaces and huffs. "Just come back to the band, Steph. We'll figure it out."

I'm not too sure what he means, but when I glance between the guys, my skin crawls and my arm aches. "I don't know," I say softly.

"Come on, princesa. We all want you back. The fans want you back." Adrian gestures toward me. "I know damn well you miss it, too."

He holds my gaze as I gnaw on the inside of my lip. Just like last night, and probably like all the other times, I don't want to tell him no.

And, hell, I don't want to say no.

"Okay."

A grin bursts onto his face the same time Shannon grunts a victorious, "Fuck yeah."

Zak, however, scoffs loudly. "Seriously? After six years together you still can't say yes to me, but you'll say yes to my brother just fine."

My brows furrow. "Z, what the fuck do you want from me? You want me in the band or not?"

The savage heartbreak that shattered Zak's expression on stage at New Year's Ball reappears. "I want you back in the band, and I want you to be my wife." Zak shakes his head and looks away. "Maybe I'll just give him your engagement ring and you'll say yes then, huh?"

My chest bottoms out—I can't breathe. Tears sting my eyes.

My lips part, but nothing comes out.

Zak has been crying out for me this whole time.

My dry tongue attempts to wet my bottom lip. The crack that reopened splits my chest in half, letting almost two years' worth of pent-up agony bleed out.

I can't muster anything above a whisper. "You still have it?"

The front door swings open and bangs against the wall.

Robbie's glare sweeps over us. "What's up?"

"Perfect," Shannon grumbles.

Robbie crosses his arms. "Fuck's goin' on?"

Shannon sighs, staring at Robbie with petulance and pursed lips. "Band meeting."

"Oh, yeah? So why's Steph here and I'm not?"

"You're out of the band, Rob."

My jaw drops at the same time as Robbie's. "*What?*"

"That wasn't part of the deal!" I pipe up, still gaping at Shannon. "What the hell, Shan?"

Shannon's glare cuts to me. "This doesn't concern you."

"No," I interrupt. "We're not Timeless without *all* of us."

Shannon completely ignores me. "You're out, bro," he reiterates. "It's been a great run, but it's time to part ways."

I look to Dree and Z for help, but they're both too focused on Shannon and Robbie to notice.

His nostrils flare, hands ball up into fists, and the tips of his ears flush pink. "You can't do this. I made a deal."

My eyes widen. "What deal?"

"I made a deal with the devil for this goddamn band!" Robbie yells. He moves toward us, and Adrian jumps up from the couch and in front of me. "I got bloody for some stupid ritual bullshit to keep Timeless going, and this is how y'all repay me? By fucking kicking me out?"

My eyes shatter wide open and my jaw drops. "*You're* the one behind the sacrifice on the bridge?"

"Yeah," Robbie says lifelessly, looking between Adrian, Shannon, and Zak. "I did that shit so you'd come back to the band and I'd still be here for it." He jabs a finger at each of the guys. "I did something none of y'all would bother doing for Timeless. You couldn't kick me out even if you wanted to."

Shannon rises from his seat, face reddened as a flicker passes through his eyes. "It's not that we wouldn't do it—it's that you went behind our backs and did something that puts us all in danger."

"Maybe y'all shouldn't have shut me out from everything the second after Stephani left," Robbie bellows. "I'm doing what I have to to keep us together and going."

"You don't know what the fuck you're doing, Rob," Adrian sneers. "I love you, bro, but you barked up the wrong fuckin' tree."

Robbie storms forward, his face turning beet red as he growls, "Then don't shut me out, *bro*."

Adrian shoves Robbie away, and Robbie pushes back.

Adrian punches Robbie right in the gut, repeating Friday night all over again as they tumble to the floor.

Zak somehow looks even paler and watches with empty eyes, like he's given up.

"What the fuck is going on?" I shout in the middle of their brawl.

When Zak's crestfallen gaze meets mine, my heart sinks, diving into the dark and icy pit of my stomach.

I don't know what they've gotten themselves into, but I'm going to get to the bottom of it.

I lean over the center cushion, closing the space between us, and I kiss him; I kiss the guy I should've said yes to on stage at New Year's Ball in front of thousands of people.

It's like the clock turned back and instead of Robbie and Adrian grunting from wailing on each other, Shannon shouting at them to quit their shit, it's my favorite crowd on my favorite day of the year cheering and hooting and hollering because I said yes.

With the way Zak kisses me back, cool lips warming on mine with his beard brushing against my chin, it's like he's right there with me under the stage lights, reveling in the moment we never got to have.

I force myself away from Zak before tears slip over the brim and onto my cheeks, whispering, "I love you."

I run for the open door.

"Steph, wait!"

The front door slams behind me first, then the car's. I shove the key in the ignition and back away from Shannon's truck.

White feathers flutter in the periphery, highlighting a figure in the darkened trees surrounding the entrance.

Wings flap and an owl lands on the brick pillar on the left-hand side of the driveway.

I get a better look when I slow down: long black hair

appears, and so do some of Kris's features surrounding an ivory beak.

Another set of headlights flash over the trees, prompting me to bypass Kris and turn right.

Kris follows, wings beating the air to keep up.

The gash on my arm pulsates, snapping muscle sinews like dried twigs. My nerves flare and sizzle as if I sawed off my arm and slapped it across a smoking-hot grill.

Blood soaks the gauze and gushes down my arm, the crimson streams disappearing into the black material of my Timeless shirt and dripping onto my thigh.

With Kris still following and a set of headlights glaring in the rearview, I grit my teeth and grip the steering wheel tighter.

The road to home passes by on the left.

The bridge is just ahead.

I veer onto the side of the road, quickly parking and abandoning the car to make the trek through dead brush and thorny mesquite to the abandoned approach.

Tires screech behind me until grass crunches. A door slams shut.

"Steph, don't fucking go up there!"

I run to Devil's Bridge.

CHAPTER 30

LOVE YOU LIKE I DO

–VANCOUVER SLEEP CLINIC

EVERY SINGLE SCRATCH, WELT, AND SCRAPE RENEWS and reopens with each step closer to the approach.

My flesh is on fire. Blood drips down my arm to the baked earth below, and my muscles scream for me to stop.

Wings flap overhead, passing over me as Kris heads south.

I'm not letting that bitch kill me, and I'm not letting the devil take us all down.

"Stephani!"

A branch catches the blood-soaked bandage on my arm and easily snatches it off. Blood spurts down my arm. Dead grass crunches underfoot as I push forward, ignoring the thorns that tug my flesh open.

Thunder rolls above.

Lightning streaks across the sky the moment I see the approach.

White wings thrash above it.

"Kris!" I yell, feet pounding the approach. "Kris, we're ending this *tonight*, you understand?"

Fear tugs my bones backward, back toward the safety of

dead brush instead of facing Death herself as she perches on a branch above, but I force my legs forward.

Even though I'm standing a few feet away and could probably make a run for it before she can grab me, fear finally catches up with me and sends my stomach roiling as we stare at one another. Her hair is just as long as it is normally, but her eyes are pitch black and glimmer in what little light is left in the sky as lightning flashes above.

Her beak is perfectly ivory tonight, so she must have just changed.

"Who's watching Drea if Shannon's out on business and you're pulling your bullshit tonight, huh?" I question angrily.

Her beak opens and a blood-curdling screech pierces my eardrums.

My eyes widen and I take a few steps back. I trip over something huge and solid, falling backward.

My knees are raised to my chest. When I reach out, prickly fur jabs my skin.

I jolt backwards until I hit the concrete side of the approach.

My hand automatically covers my gaping mouth to contain a gasp, but that's when I feel it: my hands are covered in something slick.

The scent of wet dog and death hits me as the taste of musky copper coats my lips.

An awful retch grips my stomach as I quickly rub my palms over my shirt and shorts to wipe the blood off my hands.

"Steph, what the fuck are you doing?"

I scream, cowering further against the concrete. Wetness seeps into the seat of my shorts as my eyes focus on the approaching figure.

Zak's brows furrow, and his lips part. "Oh, Jesus."

Kris shrieks again.

"What the fuck do you want?" I yell at her as I race to stand. I can't stop wiping my hands on material—I'm covered, soaked in my own blood and some poor animal's. "I'm not fucking dying, so if that's what you want, you can forget it, bitch!"

"Stephani."

The eerie calm in Zak's voice sets all my nerves on high alert. My heart pounds against my sternum, and tears cloud my vision that I can't blink away.

"Stephani," he repeats, his dark eyes wide and focused far too intently on me to just be in shock from the amount of blood I'm covered in.

He's not staring *at* me—more like ogling.

"You need to leave."

My mouth opens and closes as I glance between Kris and Zak and rub my damp fingers together. "Are you gonna take care of her?"

"*Leave,*" he roars in a voice far deeper than normal.

I turn to run, but my feet slip on slimy concrete. I fall face first into Zak's feet and quickly clamber to get away.

A hand grabs my arm and yanks me back.

"Ow!" I yelp from the gash in my arm tearing further apart as pain rages into my shoulder.

Zak squats beside me, examining my grisly arm in his hands like a piece of steak at the butcher counter. His fingers are gentle as they drag through my blood. He rubs them together, bringing it closer to study the viscosity like he's never seen such a substance before.

Then, he stuffs his bloodied fingers into his mouth.

His eyes flutter closed; he sighs in content and sucks his fingers clean.

My eyes shatter wide open, realization knocking the breath out of my lungs.

"Zak, no," I beg in a whisper.

He brings my arm to his mouth and licks the gore, tonguing lacerated flesh that oozes maroon liquid.

I shudder at the sensation, like a cat licking with a sandpapery tongue, but I stay as still as I can—if I don't fight, maybe he'll come to his senses and stop, let me run for help.

"Zak, honey," I whisper.

He moans, still lapping up blood from my wound.

Grimacing with fresh tears renewing, I suck in a sharp breath. "Hon, please stop."

But he doesn't.

Slowly, as gently as I can possibly manage, I pull my arm back.

Zak growls and hurls me into the concrete below.

My head bashes against concrete. A pounding ache punches into my nose and forehead from the force.

His teeth sink into my torn flesh, ripping up scabs and tearing open vessels until blood gushes fresh into his mouth.

I smack his shoulder as hard as I can. "Zak!" I cry. "Stop! Jesus Christ, Z, you're hurting me!"

My head throbs from the effort, and I fall back with a whimper.

Zak crawls and straddles me, keeping his mouth firmly latched onto the wound.

I drive my fist into his hard abdomen, but he doesn't even flinch.

Everything hurts.

I make another fist, but it trembles from the effort and sends a searing blaze through my nerves.

It falls to Zak's thigh. I slap him as hard as I can, but he goes on biting and sucking like I'm not here, like there's not someone beneath him struggling to get him to stop.

White wings flap behind Zak.

My attention dawdles over to the trees above.

Kris soars over us, heading north—heading home, I guess, since Zak seems to be her dirty work for her.

I take a deep breath, two for good measure, and drive my knee up into where it will definitely hurt.

He hisses and slams me down, driving my skull into concrete.

I cry out when sharp teeth pierce the flesh of my neck.

"Zak!" I wail, trying with all my might to hit him, but he captures my arms and pins them down.

Not like I have anything left to give.

When I move, nothing happens—the strength I thought I had is lost somewhere between Zak's stomach, the concrete below, and the pounding in my head making my vision flash with the lightning above.

Tears burn my flesh from the corners of my eyes into my ears.

Zak's beard scratches as his tongue greedily laps up blood spilling from my neck.

Thunder rolls.

Even though the concrete has been soaking up the blistering Texas sun all day, it's freezing cold.

A few droplets of rain dot my forehead. They're cool and send a weak shiver down my spine.

Lightning blazes.

His grip eases on my arms, enough to where I can finagle and wrap my fingers around his hand posted above my head to squeeze with what little energy I have left.

"Zak," I cry weakly. A soft sob tumbles out, almost resembling a sad chuckle. "Hey, Chiquito."

The suction on my neck stops.

Zak slowly leans back, enough so he can peer up at my face. Blood pours from between his lips.

He gasps and trips over himself to get away.

It's so dark, but lightning bursts overhead and highlights

all the blood dribbling down his bearded chin and soaking into his shirt.

Zak looks down and cries out sharply before looking at me. "Oh, God, babe… What did I do to you?"

Lights flash in the branches overhead.

"Zak! Steph!"

My vision goes black.

Footsteps rumble like machine guns in my ears until they come to a sudden stop.

"What the fuck did you do?"

Hands touch my abdomen, my face.

"Oh, God, baby." Fingers brush hair off my forehead. "Please tell me you're alive." I barely hear it under his shaking breath, "Fuck."

"Dree?" I try to muster. It comes out as high-pitched as a mosquito.

He exhales in relief. His body burns like a furnace beside me. "Baby, I'm here. I'm here," he repeats more softly, more like he's trying to reassure himself.

I blink repeatedly. My vision comes and goes, but Dree stays by my side.

Roots or branches or something crack and rip and *whoosh* through the air. Water splashes in the river below. "Fuck!"

"Shan, just get over here."

"It wasn't supposed to fuckin' be like this, man!"

Zak sobs. The harrowing sound comes closer until he's on the side opposite of Adrian. His touch is like the sun on a sunburn.

A shrill sound pierces my ears.

It's me. It's me puling like a wounded animal.

Adrian moves. "Get the fuck away from her."

Zak moves, too. "I'm staying right here."

More footsteps sound behind us, tree branches cracking until they suddenly stop. "What the fuck…?"

A sob tears through my chest and feels like I'm being split in two. "Robbie?"

There's a scramble and a tussle, Robbie pounding the concrete above my head and shoving Zak aside. But Zak shoves back.

Someone grabs me, making me groan as a body slips beneath my upper half.

Blinking, I can make out the dark silhouette of long hair cascading down and the glint of glasses as Zak bends to me. He blubbers uncontrollably in my ear.

"This is why you don't fucking go behind our backs," Shannon bellows. His voice cracks. "You and Zak both. Y'all are gonna ruin everything and kill her with your *bullshit*."

Dree's voice breaks as he cries, "Shannon, you gotta do something."

"What the fuck am I supposed to do, huh? I can't fucking do this to her. Not to Steph."

"And you think I can? Just do something!"

Shannon and Adrian and Robbie bicker, but Zak murmurs in my ear, "Babe, talk to me. Please, say something."

I can only exhale. Gulping down a deep breath, it takes far too much to whisper, "Cold. Can't see."

Zak trembles violently. "Shannon," he howls at the top of his lungs, "just fucking do it before I lose her!"

Shuffling over thunder. Hands on my body.

Sniffles. "Don't fucking lose my sister."

"Baby, hang on."

Zak sobs and sniffles. Something drips onto my forehead as his fingers gently rake through my hair—I can't be too sure it's tears or my blood.

"I'm so sorry, babe," he whispers. "I'm so fucking sorry."

He wails, the sound piercing my eardrums. His arms tighten around me as he clutches me even closer and cries into my hair.

I make myself blink, and my vision slowly creeps back in.

Shannon's face suddenly appears squarely in mine, and I flinch.

He huffs and searches the clouds that flash as lightning streaks through them. Thin trails running down the sides of his face illuminate like tiny rivers. "Steph, I don't wanna fuckin' do this. Out of everyone, you're my ride or die. You're Mama Number Two to my little girl. You're my best friend."

He suddenly grabs me, pulling me close enough to where I can see him clearly through my darkening vision. "I am *not* about to let you go. Not like this. You hear me?"

A hot tear streaks from the corner of my eye, down my cheek. "I don't wanna die," I weep. Not now—not like this.

Shannon gently lays me back in Zak's arms. Adrian grabs my hand, Robbie the other.

Robbie presses the back of my hand to his cheek and sobs. "Don't fuckin' leave me, Steph. You can't. You're not allowed to."

I sob softly with him, what little I can muster.

Shannon studies me intently. "Stephani Wade, I'll make you a deal: if you rejoin Timeless, you'll get to live."

I blink slowly, and his outstretched hand comes into view. "We got a deal?"

"What's the catch?" I try to ask, but no sound comes out.

Rain weaves through the tears streaming down Shannon's face twitching with fury. His voice is low and harsh as he says through a clenched jaw, "The catch is you're making a deal with the fucking devil."

Thunder claps. Rain begins to fall.

Zak leans down to kiss my forehead. He trembles with each movement. "Take his hand, babe." An awful sound rumbles in his chest, vibrating in my head violently as it turns into a black hole without thought. "Steph, I can't…"

His sobs crash into my skull like a train wreck. "I can't... Oh, God, please."

I haven't been able to tell Zak yes yet. But as I slip further into freezing darkness, I know I have to say it now. And I say it with the last breath in my lungs.

I reach for Shannon's hand, and my world goes dark as I whisper, "Yes."

Order Anything for the Devil: The Second Deal
so you don't miss out on what happens next to Timeless!

Listen to the official playlist:
geni.us/auroragravesplaylists

Read Chapter 7 from Adrian's point of view:
Sign up for my newsletter to have bonus content delivered to your inbox:
newsletter.auroragraves.com

ACKNOWLEDGMENTS

There was a day when 14-year-old me I realized I was a shitty singer and definitely could not be a rock star vocalist like I'd dreamed about. I think it might've been a few days later that I picked up a pen and notebook and started writing about being a rock star, living out my fantasy on the fictional stage and obsessively writing about it between writing interviews with musicians to share on MySpace.

Anything for the Devil is based on that very first novel, so the first acknowledgement I'd like to make is to you, dear reader. Here we are 17 years later and you're holding the product of my 14-year-old self's dream. Thank you for reading—I hope you love Timeless as much as I do.

Thanks to some special friends who have been with me from the very beginning. The Three Musketeers for dealing with my wild and annoying authorial shenanigans. Chevelle, for being one of the first fans when I let some friends in freshman Spanish read the WIP; for beta reading 16 years later and willingly being scared by la lechuza. Ben, for always encouraging me to keep doing the damn thing when I wanted to quit (and did for the longest time). And Jenny for proofreading and being one of my biggest cheerleaders through this whole thing.

My eternal gratitude to Mr. Graves who eventually married that weird girl that always had headphones on her ears and a pen and notebook in hand. For being my biggest supporter, my sounding board, and listening to the wild conversations I have with myself as I try to figure out my writing. Without getting grossly over-affectionate in my first book: I love you more.

Huge thanks and appreciation to my Writing Bitches, Michelle and Amanda, for not only helping me refine this fucker, but for all the support through the good days and bad days. Thank you for being the original Team Adrian vs. Team Zak—it brings me great joy every time I sit down to write.

Lastly, and definitely not the least, I'd like to acknowledge the role music has played in the creation of *Anything for the Devil*. Really, without music, I wouldn't be writing at all. My biggest thanks to Avenged Sevenfold for almost single-handedly fueling the New Year's Ball universe.

About the Author

Aurora Graves is the author of Southern Gothic romance featuring leading dudes covered in tattoos and the women they worship. Writing gritty Southern dark romance featuring her obsessions—rock stars, local legends, and folklore—in sweltering atmospheric settings with a healthy dash of spice makes her heart sing.

Aurora is usually holed up in her office, always playing alternative and industrial metal music (usually the same song on repeat because she's neurodivergent), and when she's not taking notes or plotting out a new story idea, she's reading indie romance novels, watching horror movies, or diamond painting.

Subscribe to Aurora's newsletter for news, project updates, & bonus content
newsletter.auroragraves.com

Books by Aurora Graves

Anything for the Devil

The First Deal

The Second Deal

The Final Deal

Claiming the Witch Father